A Dope Boys' Seduction

Tina J

Copyright 2018

More Books by Tina J

A Thin Line Between Me & My Thug 1-2
I Got Luv for My Shawty 1-2
Kharis and Caleb: A Different kind of Love 1-2
Loving You is a Battle 1-3
Violet and the Connect 1-3
You Complete Me
Love Will Lead You Back
This Thing Called Love
Are We in This Together 1-3
Shawty Down to Ride For a Boss 1-3
When a Boss Falls in Love 1-3
Let Me Be The One 1-2
We Got That Forever Love
Ain't No Savage Like The One I got 1-2
A Queen & Hustla 1-3 (collab)
Thirsty for a Bad Boy 1-2
Hasaan and Serena: An Unforgettable Love 1-2
We Both End Up With Scars
Caught up Luvin a beast 1-3
A Street King & his Shawty 1-2
I Fell for the Wrong Bad Boy 1-2 (collab)
Addicted to Loving a Boss 1-3
All Eyes on the Crown 1-3
I Need that Gangsta Love 1-2 (collab)
Still Luvin' a Beast 1-2
Creepin' With The Plug 1-2
I Wanna Love You 1-2
Her Man, His Savage 1-2
When She's Bad, I'm Badder 1-3
Marco & Rakia 1-3
Feenin' for a Real One 1-3
A Kingpin's Dynasty 1-3
What Kind Of Love Is This?
Frankie & Lexi 1-3
A Dope Boy's Seduction

"Put all your shit on the table." I said calmly as the two idiots who robbed an old woman in front of a store let the tears cascade down their face. They each placed a phone and keys down on the table as they prepared for their fate.

"Where's the money you took?"

"She didn't have any." I had to laugh. Who robs someone and doesn't get money, jewelry or something?

"Please don't kill us. We didn't know she was your mom and.-"

"There is no and." I said and stood in front of them.

"Whether she was my mother or not, why the fuck you out here robbing anyway? Your brother works for me." Neither of them said a word. I looked over to the brother who had nothing to say.

"It's a shame he's about to witness this." His brother Tariq tried to put his head down but I made security keep it up.

I placed his brothers hand on the edge of the table so his wrist would hang. He tried to squirm but with the dude holding his arm, there was no way he could. I lifted my hand, looked at security to move and came down hard with my custom-made machete.

"Got damn. That's fucking disgusting." My brother Fazza said after his hand flew off and hit the ground. Blood squirted out just like in the movies.

Yes, we're twins and somewhat identical. The only way you could tell us apart, is by his eyes. He has one hazel and one blue. The shit is scary as hell if you ask me. We used to call him Crazy Eyes back in the day and he hated it but guess what, he used that shit with the ladies to this day. Those dumb bitches loved his ass too; even though he treated them like shit.

One time this nigga had two girlfriends and all three of them lived together. The women were bad as hell too. It was every man's dream but eventually, turned into a nightmare. Needless to say, the shit didn't work out because when he fucked one, the other always got jealous. He'd have to break up fights, at least four times a week. Hey, if they let him do it, I ain't judging.

Now back to the situation in front of me. The real reason I chopped this kid hand off isn't because he robbed my mother. To be honest, the lady wasn't even related to me but it was the principle. I'm a business man who has a lot of money rolling in off the streets and didn't need the cops investigating a motherfucking thing. They start asking questions and people start volunteering information they shouldn't, which will then stop the cash flow and I can't have that going on.

"What's your name?" I asked the other kid who literally peed on himself.

"Lucky."

"LUCKY!" Me and my brother busted out laughing.

"Your ass ain't lucky today my nigga." I took my gun out and shot him in the leg. None of the soldiers moved, not even Tariq, whose brother hand I chopped off.

"Listen here gentlemen." I walked around the small room we were in and studied the body language and facial expressions of each individual in here. They were all terrified and its exactly the way I wanted it.

"The moral to this story is; I allow all of you to eat very well. Therefore, none of your siblings should be robbing anyone. Now some of you may think because you're the one standing on the corner, and you're the one staying up all night, why should they get anything?" I heard a few mumbles.

"That may be true, however; your family should never, ever go without. If the bills are paid, food in the fridge and they have clothes on their back; there's no need to steal."

"Can I get a doctor please?" Lucky said. The other kid was barely keeping his eyes open, due to the amount of blood loss from his hand. I ignored him and kept talking as if both of them weren't leaking blood all over my floor.

"There may be some knuckleheads running around but the reason most people steal is because they're without something." I lifted the kids head up.

"What's your name?"

"Rahsaan." He said barely above a whisper. I guess losing blood does make you delirious.

"Rahsaan huh? Tell me what's missing in your house?"

"Food. We haven't had any for a week and the first isn't until next Tuesday." He said and it only fueled my anger.

"Get them in the back to see the doctor." I kept one on call for reasons like this. See, I tried not to kill too many

8

people unless it's necessary. I did make sure to leave them with a constant memory of how not to fuck with me.

"TARIQ! FRONT AND MOTHERFUCKIN CENTER!" I yelled out to the kids' brother. He came towards me and I beat the shit outta him. Once I finished, I kneeled down and lifted his head.

"Never see your family without because you're trying to politic with bitches. Pussy comes and goes but your family, will always have your back." I slammed his head in the ground. I knew what he did mostly with his money because after he completed his job, the first place he'd run to is the strip club. It didn't bother me because my money was right. Now here is brother without a hand, all because he couldn't put at least a hundred dollars' worth of food in the house. Trifling and stingy ass motherfucker.

"Let this be a lesson to all of you." I looked at them again.

"Don't lose a family member being greedy and selfish. If a nigga will steal from old people, he'll steal from you and there's no sympathy for someone who's late with my money." I picked the towel up and wiped down my machete.

"Ahhhhhhh." You heard someone scream out in the back.

"Someone is gonna need a prosthetic." Fazza said laughing and walked in the back to see what was going on.

"Get this nigga off my floor and send one of those bitches from downstairs to suck my dick. I need to release myself ASAP." The security guards lifted Tariq by his legs and drug him out. The rest of the crew followed suit quietly. They've seen me in action enough times to know not to say a word. I walked upstairs to one of the offices.

Today has been a crazy day. I thought to myself when one of the regulars came in to give me exactly what I wanted. She was a bad one too, but I stuck to my *head only* motto with these bitches.

The women who worked here were always willing to fuck with me or my brother. Me, however, I used them for head and nothing else. I don't need no strung-out bitches on payroll. They get too messy and I'll kill a bitch whole family for messing with my money.

I don't trust no fucking body but my brother and its gonna stay that way. I don't even trust my own girl and that's fucked up because we've been together for six years. I'm not saying she's cheating or anything, I just know with the way things have been going on between us over the last few years, there's no need to start confiding in her now.

"Hurry the fuck up. I got shit to do." She sucked her teeth but did what I said. This is the life! I laid back on the chair and let her suck all my kids out, more than once. If I wasn't fucking, the least she could do is allow me to feel those tonsils a few times. I know, I ain't shit but the bitches can't get enough.

****

"Remember the kid whose hand you chopped off?" Fazza asked as we sat there counting money.

"Which one?" Yea, I've cut a few hands off people. I don't make it a habit but it has happened a few times.

"Tariq's brother."

"Oh yea, shorty who robbed the old woman. Why?" I placed the money in the counter and listened to the machine make that wonderful noise of counting.

"His mom wants to talk to you."

"Me!" I turned to look at him.

"Yea."

"What the fuck for? She knows who we are and the consequences of fucking up." I wasn't lying though. Everyone knew of me and my brother. Most parents didn't want their kids working for us because they knew if anything went wrong the repercussions would be bad.

"How she gonna stop me in the store, assuming I was you. Had the fucking nerve to ask if we could pay for his medical bills. I told her, we did when he got that free prosthetic he rocking." I busted out laughing.

"Nah, fuck that. Does she know how much those things costs? We should take it outta Tariq pay."

"I ain't thinking about that woman. If I run into her, then we'll speak but I'm not going to look for anyone." We sat there and continued counting our money without a care in the world. Really, we didn't have any at the moment. We weren't beefing with anyone and from the looks of things we had more than enough money to last a lifetime or two. I'm not bragging but it is, what it is.

After we finished counting, I looked at the clock and it was way past two in the morning. Riley, is gonna flip the fuck out like usual. You would swear, I had ten side chicks, a few other women I considered wifey and maybe eight kids. I keep telling her its not that serious and if she doesn't stop accusing me, we finished. But like everything else I say; the shit goes in one ear and out the other. Like now, I'm walking in the house and she's sitting in one of those sports chairs people use at football games with a glass of wine in her hand.

"Where you been?" This the shit I'm talking about. No hello, how was your day, nothing.

"You know where I been Riley because you called me seven times and drove by the spot quite a few times." She sucked her teeth. Fazza spotted her on the camera and just shook his head. He couldn't stand her and trust that the feelings

13

were reciprocated. And before people assume, no they never slept together.

Fazza has a way of spotting grimy, sheisty, manipulative and fake people as he says a mile away. According to him, Riley wasn't this way in the beginning but over the years he felt she changed. I can't say she didn't because when we met, I was broke or should I say just coming up in the game. She stayed by my side and never complained about the late nights or anything else pertaining to me getting money.

Once the cash started rolling in and we took over, she became more clingy and needy and not for attention. She wanted money every time she left the house, regardless if she still had some from the previous day. If we were at the club, she stayed up under me just to show women I was off limits.

That wasn't a problem because I'm not into cheating on a woman who held me down from the very beginning. Not saying, I cheat at all but why would I dip out when she had the whole package at home? Yea, I get my dick suck here and there but its nothing to me. No woman can ever tell Riley she laid down with me. You would think she appreciated that being side chicks and mistresses loved to mention how they fucked their man, but nope. It was always something.

Riley was beautiful in all aspects, except that attitude and her recent change of being territorial. Don't get me wrong, I loved the whole that's my man thing but she went overboard more than I care to admit. I'm talking about coming in the bathroom with me at the club because she thought a chick would follow me in there. Or even showing up at meetings I'd have with the team. I can't tell you how many times Fazza would cuss her out, then I'd have to get in his ass over it and still have to deal with it at home. Riley felt he should've never been comfortable addressing her but what did she expect? That's my brother and I'd do the same.

Anyway, Fazza felt that once the money started rolling in all she wanted to do was spend her time shopping and clocking my moves. Its true but again, being she held me down I allowed her to be a stay at home chick. Unfortunately, in doing so, her ass had way too much time on her hands and the shit is starting to irk my fucking nerves.

"Ok but we were supposed to go out for dinner."

"Since when?"

"Since I text you earlier and you never responded."

"If I didn't respond then obviously I didn't see it." I began to walk up the spiral staircase in this four thousand square foot mansion she had to have, when I felt something on the back of my neck. I didn't realize what it was until the glass shattered all over the steps and onto the ground. I rubbed my temples and slowly walked towards her.

This is another issue Fazza didn't like about her. She had a serious hand problem when things didn't go her way. I usually let it slide but from blood trickling down my neck, ain't no way I'm letting her get away with this.

Watching Mazza come towards me pumped no fear in my heart whatsoever. See, he and I have been together so long that I've learned he had a weakness and that weakness, is me. Not only have we been a couple for six years, but I was the first woman he fell in love with. The first woman he went down on and the first woman, who stuck around when his ass had no money.

Of course, he had those little teenage hos' running after him but none of them tried to be around too long because he was broke. However, Mazza had a fire in him and I knew that from the very beginning. He was motivated by the power Shakim had in the streets before someone killed him.

Shakim was a legend and had a shit load of money. Bitches were at his beckon call and did any and everything for him; including me. No one knew I was his woman because he kept me hidden away. This man had a mean streak outta this world and I hated to witness it. Unfortunately, I did on more than one occasion and sometimes couldn't see or move for days and one time, two weeks. He'd always say I was cheating or plotting on him. How could I do either when I was stuck in the house?

He even alienated me from my family, who at the time tried to get him locked up because of my age. Shit, Shakim was thirty and I was only sixteen. Yes, I was hot in the ass and thought it would be cute to be with and older man. Well it was fine and dandy until he realized he was my first. After that, things went downhill. He did teach me a lot in the bedroom though, which I brought in my relationship with Mazza who was strung out in my eyes. No one could hold a torch with me in the bedroom and he knew it.

Anyway, Shakim had the twins under his wing and taught them everything. I didn't meet them because he never brought anyone to the house, and if he did I had to stay in the room and not make a noise. He thought everyone would want me but I think it was more of a control thing. My man was crazy like that.

The streets began to respect the twins as if they were him and to be honest, its how he wanted it. He said, his time was coming to an end and they would be his successors because everyone else he tried out, failed. I didn't know at the time but Shakim had the twins committing murders on some politicians, cops, lawyers and so many others, that people were too scared to fuck with them at all. Then there here was the no snitching rule so they never worried about getting caught.

Sadly, one night, Shakim was driving home and someone ran him off the road. His car plummeted off a cliff and it wasn't until the next day that someone found him. Evidently, the area he was in, housed a chick who had two of his children. I was devasted because one of them were only six months old, which means he cheated. I let his family deal with his arrangements and never went to the funeral. Low and behold, the day after the service I go to the store only to come back with a bitch, two kids and security blocking my doorway.

Long story short, Shakim left a will and in it, he stated that I be moved off the premises and sent back to live with my family. He left the chick everything, including his money, other houses, cars and some damn vacation houses I didn't even know about. Devasted again, I took the loss and went home.

A year later I ran into Mazza, we hit it off and been together ever since but lately, its like he doesn't wanna be around me and well I'm not having it. I worked too hard to keep him and no other bitch is gonna have me looking like a fool again.

"What did I tell you about putting your hands on me." He stood directly in front of me. Now I wasn't scared but his facial expression was different. Its like he wanted to beat my ass and that's never happened.

"Actually, I didn't hit you, the glass did." And just like that one of his hands were around my throat, while the other pushed my back against the wall. Usually, this type of behavior would insinuate rough sex but not this time.

"I let you get away with a lotta shit Riley but if you ever do that again or should I say throw anything at me again, I'm gonna forget who you are and beat the shit outta you." He said it with so much anger in his voice I was a tad bit nervous.

"Who is she?" He squeezed my throat a little tighter and let go.

"I don't know what you're talking about." He walked away and ran up the steps.

"CLEAN THIS SHIT UP!" He shouted which again is something he doesn't do with me. I eased passed the glass and made my way to the bedroom to see if he were on the phone or tryna be sneaky.

I stared as he removed his clothes, stepped outta his boxers and went in the master bathroom. Blood was trickling down his neck and to be honest, there was a gash in the back. It wasn't too bad but it will probably require a stich or two. Who knew I had that good of an aim? I picked his things up and tossed them in the basket, only to see a card drop with a woman's number on the back. I stormed in the bathroom, snatched the glass door open and waited for him to turn around.

I couldn't help but get turned on. Mazza was very handsome and his body is the kind all women craved for. I'm talking about the perfect abs, the muscles protruding everywhere and the prize possession he held in between his legs, is enough to make a bitch go crazy. Hence the reason I

21

am, the way I am towards him. Yes, I showed him a lotta freaky things in the bedroom but he turned my ass out. Say what you want, but I'm gonna be that crazy bitch because no one will ever get him.

"What's this?" He turned around and the blood was leaking on the shower floor.

"It looks like a card."

"It is with a bitch name on it. Now who is Shelby?" He laughed and turned back around. I stepped in fully dressed and all.

"Mazza, I don't wanna have to kill the bitch. I suggest you tell her…" He placed both of his hands on the wall. One on each side of my face.

"I'm not telling her shit because Shelby is a guy I plan on doing business with."

"Oh." I put my head down and attempted to step out but he caught my wrist.

"All you say is oh??" I gave him a fake smile.

"Nah, you're gonna pay for this." He pointed to his head that was still dripping. He put his palm on the top of my head and pushed me to the ground.

"I don't feel like it." I whined.

"I don't give a fuck. You acting childish over nothing and my dick hard, so do it." I wanted to protest but said fuck it. I was wrong with the card shit, but I don't take back throwing the glass at him.

"Shit, that feels good." He moaned out as I started slow and sped up some. I felt his hand on my head again and almost fell back as he rammed himself in and out my mouth harder and faster. I tried to stop him but he had a tight grip on me. I was gagging, my throat was hurting and tears started flooding my eyes.

"Got damn that was good." He pulled out and came on my face and in my hair. Sometimes we get freaky like this but only if I wanted to. He lifted me up by my hair and put his face close to my ear.

"I don't give a fuck how good this pussy is; if you ever in your fucking life throw something at me again, I'll fucking

23

kill you." He slammed my head on the wall and stepped out. Who the hell is this man? Mazza has never threatened me with any type of harm. Am I pushing him away? Is he really gonna kill me? I had to make amends fast because he had me scared.

I shut the water off and walked in the room to see a towel on his head and him putting clothes on. It was safe to assume he was going to get his head looked at. Did I feel sorry? Nope and I'd do it again. Next time, I'll make sure to run out the house. I know he told me not to do it again but he won't really kill me? Will he?

****

"Bitch. That nigga gonna kill you." My friend Evelyn said. She and I met when we were five and been best friends for the last twenty years. She knew everything about me and vice versa. She was my voice of reasoning when I listened.

"He'll be alright." I waved her off and continued looking on the rack in Saks. She and I took a ride to New York. Delaware wasn't as far but far enough when you don't wanna take the ride.

"Look at me Riley." She swung me around.

24

"Honey, you're losing yourself in him." I folded my arms.

"What you mean?"

"I'm saying. You don't work, sit at home all day, ride around stalking him, you put your hands on him and now you're throwing objects at him. You need a hobby. Get outta the house and get a job or something."

"A job? Bitch, are you crazy?" She chuckled like what I said was funny.

"No, I'm being realistic with you. That man has dealt with a lotta shit from you over the years and from the things you're telling me, he seems to be getting fed up." She took both of my hands in hers.

"Riley, I don't want you to end up on the street with nothing again."

"Really?"

"Yes really. You know as long as I have a place, you will too but don't let it get that far. Start working and…" I cut her off.

"I have money saved for a rainy-day Evelyn. I'm not that stupid." She laughed shaking her head.

"Sweetie, your man has so many connections its ridiculous. You think he doesn't know about those secret bank accounts or the shit you have at your parents' house?"

"No he can't."

"Never underestimate a man. Especially; one who has a gold digging, abusive girlfriend."

"Bitch."

"What? Its what you are." She shrugged her shoulders.

"You don't have to say it."

"Why not? Maybe if you hear it, you'll get your shit together." I hated listening to Evelyn but she was right. I needed to get a job and occupy my time. My mom always said never to depend on a man and that's exactly what I've been doing. Hopefully, Mazza will appreciate this because Lord knows I don't even have skills to do shit. College was never in my future and I damn sure ain't working at McDonalds.

"Don't stress Riley. You can work at my job."

"I didn't say anything."

"You don't have to. I know you didn't go to college and you're too good to work at fast food places." We both started laughing.

"What will I do at your job?" Evelyn went to college and opened her own marketing firm. At first, she wasn't making any money but once her business took off, it really took off. My girl was raking in big money, including some from the twins. They had business around the state and in others and she ran all types of ads, and even job fairs for them. Shit, the least she can do is get me a job.

"You'll be in the mailroom."

"Oh hell no." I was against that shit.

"Riley, you have to start at the bottom."

"Why?"

"Because regardless if its my business or not, everyone there knows you're my best friend. I can in no way possible start you at the top with no degree." I rolled my eyes and told her I understood.

"I am going to have you enrolled in the classes to become a manager and even sign you up for business classes online."

"I don't know Evelyn. It seems like a lot."

"I know but I'll be there to help you." She gave me a hug and told me everything was going to be ok. I had to take it one day at a time and not stress over the small things or I'd drive myself crazy. I hope she's right because I don't know how long I can work in some mailroom. Shit, I may as well be a cashier somewhere.

"I told yo ass to leave that bitch alone." I told my twin who was sitting in my house with this new girl Tyler I met, stitching him up. She stopped by after work to bring me some food and we got to talking before my brother came.

She's a nurse and the two of us been spending a lotta time together. Not that I want to but she bad as hell and a nigga tryna fuck. Sad to say, she ain't giving it up and making me work for her ass. I would assume after thirty days she'd give it up but not her. We damn near known each other for two months and she still pretending to be celibate.

"Aye. What I tell you about that?" He barked and I put my hands up in surrender. He hated when I spoke ill of Riley but shit, she's a bitch who is only with my brother for his money.

"A'ight nigga. You always get so damn sentimental when it comes to her." Tyler looked over at me.

"What?"

"Nothing." She said and poured some solution on his head.

"Hi Mazza. I'm Tyler and it's nice to meet you."

"Oh shit. My bad. Tyler this my twin if you can't tell. And Maz, this is Tyler. She the new chick I'm tryna fuck."

"WHAT?" She barked and turned to look at me.

"I mean, tryna get to know. Calm yo hostile ass down."

"Nigga, don't let my pink scrubs, crocs and nursing license fool you. We can get it popping in this bitch."

"And don't let these pretty eyes fool you. I'll..."

"You'll what nigga?" She went in that little black bag she has her medical stuff in and pulled out a taser.

"What the fuck is that gonna do?"

Zzzzzz. Zzzzzz. My body jerked and I hit the floor.

"Thanks for stitching me up." I don't know how long I was out but I woke up still on the floor, and heard my brother thanking her. I hopped up fast as hell.

"You finally woke up huh?" She had the nerve to say.

"Bitch."

"Bitch?"

"Damn right I said bitch. I wish you would tase me again." I took my piece out and placed it on her temple. She stood there with her arms folded and a smirk on her face.

"Yo, I'm out. Y'all motherfuckers doing too much. Nice to meet you Tyler and thanks for stitching me up." Maz said on his way out.

"Bro, you really let her tase me?" He turned around.

"The way I see it is, you finally met your match." He closed the door and Tyler started picking her things up to leave.

"Where the fuck you going?"

"Away from your crazy ass." She tried to walk past me and I snatched her ass up.

"Nah. After that tasing shit, you got two choices."

"You bugging."

"Ain't nobody bugging. Like I said, you got two choices."

"And they are?"

"One... you can ride my dick or suck it; whichever you choose. Or two... I can splatter your brains all over this couch."

"So you'll mess your couch up if we don't get it popping?"

"Option one or two." I put my finger on the trigger and cocked the gun.

"Let me think about it and get back to you." She turned to leave and I let one off in the back of her leg.

"Oh my God. Are you serious?"

"Yea. I thought about what you said and I don't wanna mess up my couch. Now get the fuck out." I opened the door and watched her cry.

"Fazza, I swear to God if you don't take me to the hospital I'm gonna break your dick when I ride it." I grabbed my shit because it sounds like it hurt.

"Ughhhhh, why can't you take yourself?" I grabbed my keys and walked out.

"FAZZA!" I stopped and turned.

"WHAT?"

"I can't walk you fucking asshole."

"Whose fault is that?" I went towards the door.

"I better not have to take a leave of absence because of this. If I do you're paying all my bills."

"The fucking lies you tell." I lifted her up and carried her to the car.

"Stay right here." I ran in my house, grabbed a few towels and locked up.

"Hurry up. I'm losing a lotta blood."

"Really?" She had the nerve to get mad looking at the towels.

"Hell yea. Ain't no way in you're about to bleed all over my shit."

"Fazza, we are done after this. Drop me off and never look back."

"Shut yo dramatic ass up. Always talking shit." I placed the towels under her leg and sped to the hospital. She called on the way over so two nurses were standing outside.

"You cry ugly." I told her as they helped place her on a stretcher.

"God, why is this man in my life?"

"Because you wanna ride this big ass dick. He had to make sure you got a taste of what these bitches bugging over." The black nurse was hysterical laughing and the white one turned beet red.

"Please don't let him be here when I wake up."

"Oh, I won't be. This other bitch calling so I'm gonna fuck her and come back to check on you. K." I pecked her lips and she swung off, almost catching me in the face.

"Save that violence for when I have you up against the wall taking all this dick."

"Oh my God. GET OUT AND DON'T COME BACK." She yelled and I hit her with the peace sign.

"Take care of her y'all. I need that pussy energized when I get in it." I lifted my pants from sagging and jogged out the door. Hell yea I'm about to hit the bitch off that called.

****

"Shit, I need this dick in my life everyday." My ex bitch Shanta said. I call her that because it's what she is. When we were together all she did is nag and complain so I cheated numerous times on her. Call me what you want but she

34

deserved it. I mean a nigga tried to be faithful but since she kept accusing me I went out and did it. That way, I could say she was right.

"Too bad. You had it and blew it."

"I didn't blow it too bad. You still pay my bills and give me the dick when I want it."

"True but when I get a new bitch, the supply will be cut off." She fell into a fit of laughter.

"Oh it's funny?"

"Hell yea. You can't be faithful to save your life."

"I'm offended." I stood to put my jeans on.

"You shouldn't be. You're a dog and always will be." She pulled the sheet over her body and stood up.

"Let's be clear Shanta. I was faithful to you until the accusations started. After a while, it became nonstop so I gave you what you wanted."

"Excuse me." She had her hands on her hips.

"You wanted me to cheat so I did. I mean it's the only reason I could come up with as to why you kept accusing me."

"I was in love with you Fazza. Hell, I still am. I never wanted you to dip out and it was my own insecurities that had me thinking crazy shit. I messed up but you could've left me alone and slept with other people." She had sadness in her eyes.

"But then I'd be alone. What kinda sense did that make?"

"I fucking hate you."

"Wait! I thought you said you're still in love with me. You can't have it both ways." I slid my shirt over my body.

"I hate that sarcasm but I love everything else about you. The way you sleep, talk, pick your hair out."

"Yo, that's creepy as hell. You could've at least said the way I fuck you." I pushed her gently towards the wall.

"We both know it's what you miss the most." I felt her leg sliding up and down mine.

"Umm hmm. What I tell you? Daddy, got that dope dick." She tried to stick her hand in my jeans.

"I'm good."

"Fazza stop playing."

"I'm not. I have to go check on the Mrs."

"The Mrs.?" She questioned with an attitude.

"Yea I don't wanna be single forever. Plus, this chick got in my head and we haven't even fucked yet."

"So how she the Mrs.?"

"Because she smart as hell, can cook her ass off, and took good care of me one day when I was sick. All I need to see now is if the pussy good. If it is, the Fazza dick train stops here. Peace." I kissed her cheek and went down the steps. I heard her yelling for me to come back.

I jumped in my car, went home to shower and go back to the hospital. I meant what I said about Tyler. So far she's the full package. If the sex good, it's a wrap for these ho's.

I opened my eyes and this crazy motherfucker was asleep on the chair. I picked up a pillow and threw it at him. Why in the hell is he here and did he not hear me scream not to come back? No he heard me, he just didn't listen.

"Why you throwing shit? You want me to shoot you in the other leg?" He smirked.

"Fazza, just go."

"Hell no. It's late as fuck outside. What if someone tries to run up on me?"

"I highly doubt you're scared."

"You never know." He stood, stretched and smiled when he saw me staring at his rock hard dick. I can't front, even through his jeans it looked like it could tear my insides up.

"Oh you're definitely gonna take a ride on it." I sucked my teeth at his confidence.

"Let me piss first and we can discuss how this thing is gonna work." He pointed between the two of us.

"Ain't shit working because..."

"Yea, yea. Save all that." He left me with my mouth opened while he used the bathroom. I reached over to get my cell off the table. Before they put me under, I asked that my phone be here and not in my bag. Knowing the pain would be bad, I wouldn't be able to get up.

I looked at the missed calls from my mom who was expecting me to stay the night. She and I always had girls' night on Saturday's. It's like a ritual we had since my father passed away two years ago from a heart attack. He never had heart problems and one day he woke up, went to the bathroom and passed out. They say it was a massive one and nothing would've saved him.

We were both devastated because we've always been close. When you lose someone in the circle, the gap will never be filled.

I hit send and waited for her to answer. It was after one in the morning but she'll still pick it up.

"Tyler are you ok?" Yes, I had a boy's name. That's because the doctors told my parents I was a boy all the way up until she pushed me out. They loved the name and had nothing else picked out. My father said it's like he had his son by the name even though I was a girl. And no, he didn't push football or any other male dominating sport on me.

"I'm ok. I got shot in the back of my leg and.-" This nigga snatched the phone out my hand.

"Hi there Mrs. Evans. This is Fazza and I'm Tyler's new friend."

"Fazza? What kind of name is that?" He had her on speaker.

"I'm a twin and my brother's name is Mazza. Our parents named us that to sound similar to mother and father. I don't know why before you ask." I busted out laughing because he was lying his ass off.

I asked about his name before and he told me his mom was searching the Internet for names and back then it wasn't a lotta websites. She said, they needed a name no one would have and she saw Mazza. Since they're twins she wanted them to match.

"Well, that's different but ok. Why are you with my daughter?"

"Oh she tased me so I shot her." He said in a non chalant way.

"WHATTTTTTT!" My mom shouted.

"Yea she can't go around tasing people and not expect consequences. I know a bullet is different but I could've had heart issues. She didn't know so in my eyes, we're even."

"Oh my Lord. TYLERRRR!" She yelled not knowing she was on speaker.

"Give me the phone fool."

"Here but don't get mad at me. Shit, it's the truth." He handed me the phone and I took her off speaker.

"Yes ma."

"Are you ok? Oh my God."

"I'm good ma. It wasn't that bad."

"Tyler, your father has to be turning in his grave. Get him outta there." Fazza was cracking up because he could hear her yelling.

"I tried ma but he won't leave." I looked up and he was cheesing hard as hell. This fool had taken all his clothes off except his boxers and tank top.

41

"Move over, damn. Taking up all the space." He pushed me over and had the nerve to rest his head on my chest.

"Ma, let me call you back." She cried for me to contact the cops. What do I look like calling the cops on his crazy ass? I know exactly who he is and the type of weight him and his brothers name hold, which is exactly why I tried to stay away from him. Unfortunately, he refused to let me.

"Yo, let me get your number." I heard and turned around to stare into the eyes of this sexy ass man. He was brown skin with two different color eyes. At first, I thought it was weird until he smiled. I don't know why but it turned me on. He had a ton of tattoos and the one on his neck that read Ernestine was even sexier. I know, the weirdest things entertain me. I found out later it's his mom name.

"Is that how you ask a woman?"

"Ugh yea." He folded his arms.

"I'm not giving you my phone number with your rude ass."

"The hell you not. Stop playing I got things to do." I rolled my eyes and pushed my cart.

"YO! THIS CHICK RIGHT HERE SAID EVERYONE IN HERE IS BROKE AND SHOULD GO APPLY FOR FOOD STAMPS." My mouth dropped open as people turned around. Some had their face turned up and the old people were shaking their head.

"Will you stop it?" I tried to whisper.

"Those digits."

"No thanks." I gave him a fake smile. He went to open his mouth again.

"Ok. Ok here."

"It better be the right number. Matter of fact, stand here while I dial it." He did and my phone rang.

"What type of fucking ring tone is that?" He spoke of my nature noises.

"I love listening to the sounds of the outdoors."

"That's good to know."

"Why is that?" He put his phone back on the clip.

"So when we fuck, I know you won't mind doing it outside. You can hum along with the birds. See ya." He moved

past me and went straight out the store. That was two months ago and now I couldn't get rid of his ass.

Don't get me wrong, we have fun when we're not arguing. He loves running his hands threw my hair when I'm lying in his lap. He's stayed over a few times and even after I left for work. I come home from work now and he'll be on the couch watching sports center. Yup! This nigga made a damn key to my place. The sad part is I've already fallen hard for him and he's nowhere near ready for a relationship.

"I can't wait to get in between these legs."

"Fazza, I'm going to sleep."

"It's ok Ty. You're gonna be in love soon." I turned over the best I could.

"If only you knew." I said to myself.

✳✳✳✳✳✳✳✳✳✳✳✳✳✳

"Damn you heavy." Fazza said when he lifted me in his arms.

"Really nigga? You tryna say I'm fat?"

"Hell no. You thick as hell tho." He used his own key to open the door and sat me on the couch.

44

"Gee thanks. You can go now."

"I ain't going nowhere until you make me something to eat."

"Fazza, I can barely walk with these crutches and..."

"Stop complaining and bring one of those kitchen chairs in there to sit. I took some steak out this morning when I brought you some clothes. The least you can do is feed me." I stared at him and rolled my eyes. Since he stayed the night at the hospital, I made him come to the house and bring me clean clothes.

"Why you rolling your eyes?"

"Don't you have to meet up with your brother?"

"Later. Come on Ty. Stop playing." He stood me up and placed his face on my neck. When his lips touch it, I felt myself getting turned on. He and I never slept together or should I say have sex because he's stayed the night a lot. We pecked each other on the lips and cheek but no tongue and we've never felt the other up. Shit, I haven't even see him naked and vice versa.

"Look at me Ty." He used his index and middle finger to lift my face.

"I know you're feeling me and trust me when I say, I have feelings for you too but I got a lot going on. I don't wanna drag you into it. But when I'm ready, I promise you'll be the only woman I choose." He slid his tongue over my lips and then inside my mouth. My hands found their way around his neck and his were sliding inside the back of my jeans.

"Mmmmm. You're not ready yet." He pulled back and said before slapping my ass.

"I'm not waiting forever." I threw the crutch and walked to the kitchen on my tippy toes.

The bullet only grazed my leg and all I had on was an ace bandage and small brace. The crutches were unnecessary but I still had them.

"I won't make you wait that long but I do know, no other man will be around you." I swung my body to look at him.

"What?" He took an apple and walked out. He must be crazy if he thinks I'm sitting around waiting for him.

Ty, can play tough all she wants but ain't no man gonna be around her and I mean it. It's not that I didn't wanna be with her; it's just I'm still fucking other bitches. It wouldn't be fair to her and I definitely don't wanna hurt or even see her cry. For some reason, she had me falling hard and fast. The only way to escape it is to find others to occupy my time. The crazy thing about that is, I find myself thinking about her when I'm with them too.

"Here and lock up when you go." She placed the plate of food in front of me. The steak was well done and the mashed potatoes and string beans topped it off.

"Where you going?" I patted the seat next to me.

"I'm tired Fazza."

"Did you eat?"

"No. I wanna shower first and then I'll eat."

"Nah fuck that." I put my fork down, went in the kitchen and brought hers in the dining room.

"I'm not hungry." I put some mashed potatoes on the fork.

"Open your mouth."

"Fazza, I said. -"

"I don't care what you said Ty. You need to eat before taking medication." She opened up and took the fork from me.

"Was that hard?" I placed a kiss on her cheek.

She and I sat there eating and talking about random shit. Shorty smart as hell and even though she's an RN, she was starting school to become a physician assistant. I asked why not a doctor, and she said it's way too much work. Regardless of her choice, a nigga was impressed like a motherfucker.

"I'm full." She laid her head on my shoulder.

"I'll clean up for you." She looked at me.

"What? My mom did raise a gentleman." I thought she'd fall out the chair from laughing so hard.

"Whatever. Go shower. I wanna make sure you're good before I go."

"You staying the night?" She stood and limped toward the stairs.

"Not sure. We got some shit going on." She nodded and went upstairs.

48

I cleaned up and put the dishes in the dishwasher. Yea, my mom raised me right but I still ain't doing no damn dishes. I wiped the table and counters down.

Ty was on her way down the steps when the doorbell rang. It was only seven, which wasn't too late but still. Who the hell was coming over?

"You expecting someone?"

"Not that I know of." She had confusion on her face too.

"Better not be no nigga."

"And if it was? You ain't my man." She folded her arms.

"Get fucked up Ty." She waved me off and made her way to the door. I leaned on the wall with a toothpick in my mouth waiting to see who it is.

"Ma. What you doing over here?" I grinned because I know once she sees me, she'll have something to say.

"I came to check on you. The hospital said you were gone. Why did you leave so soon?" She stepped in and continued talking without noticing me.

49

"It was a flesh wound and I didn't need to stay long. You could've called."

"I did and it went to voicemail."

"That's because I turned it off." I said. She turned quickly and looked back at Ty.

"Is this him?" She pointed.

"Yes."

"Why is he here? Honey, you were supposed to call the cops." I picked my keys and phone up.

"If she called the cops ma'am, I'd be forced to explain how she tased me first. Therefore, the shot was me defending myself. You don't want this sexy woman in jail, do you? I mean the women would love her in there but then you'd miss her." Ty shook her head and her mom's mouth fell open.

"Anyway. It was nice meeting you Mrs. Evans. Ty, I'll see you later."

"Oh no you won't. My daughter will not deal with a street thug like you. Ty, tell him it's over." She looked up at me.

"Tell me our friendship is over Ty. I wanna hear you say it." I stood there with my arms folded but no words left her mouth. I knew she was in love with me, which is why I'm gonna make her my girl soon.

"I'll call you in a few." I leaned down and placed a soft kiss on her lips.

"She's too scared, can't you tell?" Her mom tried to push me out the door.

"She accepted that kiss tho." Her mom sucked her teeth and was about to get smart.

"Be careful Mrs. Evans. Depending on what you say next will decide how rough I'll be on her you know what." Ty covered her mouth trying not to laugh, while her mother couldn't do shit but stare. I left both of them standing there and went to my car. I had enough fun for the day. Let me get my night started.

****

"What up?" I dapped up my dude Kelly, who worked directly under me. I didn't fuck with a lot of people and the

51

only man I trusted is my brother. If I needed to pick another person to tell my secrets to, Kelly would be him.

I sat next to him and he was already drinking and bullshitting with a few other people. We did this shit every other day or when he was in some shit at home with his girl.

"Not much. About to watch some chicks shake their ass."

"Is there ever a time you don't?"

"Yea, when my girl ain't getting on my nerves."

"You been with her for eight years bro. It's what she supposed to do. And y'all got three bad ass boys together. I'm sure she need a break too." I always had to school him on some shit.

I'm not a relationship expert by any means but my mom raised two bad ass twins by herself, so I know the struggle. Kelly may live with his girl and even have his kids but women for sure needed time alone. My mom used to tell us all the time how she wished our dad was in the picture to give her a break.

I think it's why Mazza is more sentimental when it comes to women. I am too but only if she's my woman. Shit, you can't go around showing your soft side to everyone. They'll assume you're weak and I ain't got time for that. A bitch will try and get over fast.

"I know. I guess this wedding shit getting to me. How you do it? Well you don't have a chick now but still."

"Really?"

"Really. I thought you and Shanta were gonna be together, forever." He said as I had the waitress bring me a drink.

"Nah. She couldn't handle a nigga like me."

"Nigga, I don't think no bitch can." He busted out laughing. If he only knew there is one and he'll find out soon enough.

We were sitting there for an hour when Tariq stepped in with some of the guys off the block. My brother wasn't lying when he said all he does is spend time in these clubs. Between him and Kelly, I swear they were running a damn race. Not only did all the bartenders know them by name but so did the strippers. They'd run straight to them when they walked in; knowing money would be made.

Kelly sat up, as did the others who were in our section when they noticed him. One thing I never worried about was any of these dudes having my back. Its not that they were scared but they knew how good my brother and I were to them. We made sure everyone ate well and if there was a problem and they wanted to make more money, we'd figure something out. When you're good to your team, they'll remain loyal, which is why I don't understand why this punk motherfucker came and stood in front of me.

I put my arm in front of Kelly who was about to dig in his ass. I didn't need anyone fighting my battles and I wanted to know why the hell he was here anyway.

"What up Tariq?" I let my tongue shift the toothpick from the right side of my mouth, to the left.

"Nothing much boss. Can we join the party?" He said with a smirk on his face.

"Is there food in your house?" I looked him up and down.

"What?" He tried to jump bad.

"You heard what I said. But since you pretend not to, I'll repeat the question." I pushed him out my way and rose to my feet. This nigga wanna act bad so I think its time to show him what I'm working with.

"I said, is there food in your motherfucking house? Matter of fact, are all the bills paid?"

"Oh, you being funny?"

"And you think you're tough." I spit the toothpick out my mouth and watched it bounce off his forehead.

"Fuck you Fazza. You think that shit was cute Mazza did to my brother?"

"Nah, my nigga. I would never want my brother's hand cut off in front of me but then again, it would never happen and you know why?" I stepped closer. He backed up and the guys with him dispersed like I knew they would.

"Because I'd make sure my family was taken care of before spending my bread on these bitches." I waved my hand around the club.

"How the fuck you mad when its your fucking fault?"

55

"How is it my fault? I didn't tell that nigga to rob no one." This is the shit I'm talking about. Here he is, questioning me about Mazza cutting his brothers hand off, yet; saying it ain't his fault.

"Tariq, your mother is on disability. Correct?" I asked and intertwined my hands to crack my knuckles. I can see now he's gonna make me beat his ass.

"Yea why?"

"All the reason to make sure there's food in the house and the bills are paid. What type of son will make his mom wait for her food stamps to go on the card, make her bills late all because he doesn't wanna give her money?" He didn't say shit.

"Exactly! Your selfish acts made your brother go out there and rob an old woman just to eat. That's commendable because he was tryna make sure everyone ate by any means necessary. Unfortunately, he got caught and lost a hand. Where you standing here after getting off, with maybe two stacks in your pocket to blow on these bitches. How much are you giving your mother to maintain the household?"

"My family is none of your concern." He had the audacity to say.

"It is when your mother is asking if we can pay for your brothers' medical bills."

"Tariq, what the fuck is wrong with you? That's your family. You can't be that selfish and greedy." One of the guys said. We never mentioned to any of them what went on unless it concerned them but since he was being tough, I had to let him know he don't run shit.

"Nah, he is. Let me fill you in on a secret though." I put my mouth by his ear.

"Before you try and act tough, make sure you have a team behind you." He looked around.

"You see, they may have drove here with you but none of them wanna get caught up in whatever you have going on. Am I right?" I turned and they all shook their heads no.

"I suggest you find a different spot to chill in tonight." I nodded and security came to escort him out.

"This ain't over." He shouted.

"Is that a threat?" He put his hands up and that was it. I strolled over to the bottom of the steps where security dropped him at and knocked the shot outta him. I didn't wanna put him to sleep because he had me ready to fight and if he's asleep, there's no telling when he'd wake up.

"You'll really sneak me?"

"Bro, you were looking right at me. Since you're tough let's get this poppin." He swung and missed.

"Tell your mama I'm not paying for these doctors' bills either."

"What?" Is all he could get out before I beat the shit outta him. I could feel security pulling me off and when they did, Tariq looked dead. I stomped on his face a few more times and made my way out the club.

"You want me to end him?" Kelly asked as we walked to our cars.

"Nah. I think he learned his lesson and if not, he will." I hit him with the peace sign, hopped on my car and pulled off. Niggas always testing my gangsta. I bet he won't do that shit no more.

"Bro, I hate taking this drive. Why can't dude meet us?" Fazza complained on our way to Maryland. He just finished telling me about the shit with Tariq. I couldn't even feel sorry because he had no reason approaching Fazza. Then he wanted to be tough so he got what he deserved. There's always one out the bunch who wanted to try and show their masculinity or toughness. They never listen and, in the end, it never works out good for them.

Today we were going to pick up some money from the workers we had out there and meet up with this guy who wanted to start purchasing by the weight. I'm all for making money but there's no way, I'm going in blind. I needed to meet this dude, feel him out and dig deep in his background. If a person is asking for product by the weight, they're either rolling in money or the feds. Not that I'm worried because like all people high up in the food chain, law enforcement was on our side but I still like to be cautious.

Fazza on the other hand, loves to live his life on the edge and that's all fine and dandy until shit goes wrong and we go on a damn killing spree. It only happened a few times but still. I guess it's more of a pain for me because of Riley. I would have to be away for days and sometimes weeks at a time and she'd have a fit. Granted, I'd face time her and even brought gifts home but she wasn't having it. It's like she wanted to be up under me no matter what I did.

I can say as of lately, or should I say since the day she hit me in the head with a glass, she's gotten a job and hasn't been as bitchy. She even opened up her own bank account and started saving her money. Yea, I know all about the secret accounts and other hiding places she has money in. Everything she has in those accounts is what I gave her. I don't know why she doing all that because I ain't no Indian giver.

"He'll be meeting us back home soon enough."

"Good. These rides make my stomach hurt. Pull over at this Dunkin Donuts real quick." I busted out laughing because every road trip he'd have to shit and the people in the store would be mad. Let's just say Fazza doesn't smell good at all after using the bathroom.

"Hurry up."

61

"Man be quiet. Get out and grab something to eat. We have a little longer to go and you grouchy as fuck when you hungry." He ran inside before I could respond. We were in Aberdeen Maryland and the person stayed in Silver Springs. They weren't too far apart but its still a ride he hated to take.

"Hi and welcome to Dunkin Donuts. How can I help you today?" The short cashier asked and smiled.

"Let me get a big and toasty sandwich with a medium vanilla bean coolatta. Also, give me two jelly donuts and I'm gonna get this sprite." I walked over to the fridge that held the sodas in and grabbed it.

"Ok, that'll be $15.34. Is that for here or to go?"

"GOT DAMN MY STOMACH HURTS." You heard Fazza shouting in the bathroom. The cashier looked over the counter and then at me. I shrugged my shoulders and handed her the money.

As I stood there waiting for my food, I read the text Riley sent me about work. You would think since her best friend gave her a job she'd be happy and appreciative but not her. She complained about everything, from the mailroom to the lunch they served in the cafeteria. I tried to tell her to be patient but if it ain't Riley's way, it ain't no way.

"WHEW! I think y'all need a plumber in there." Fazza came out holding his stomach. Some lady that just walked in made her way to the bathroom and instead of Fazza warning her, he let her go in. The woman came right back out gagging and telling the cashier how much the bathroom stunk and needed to be cleaned. She looked straight at Fazza. Why did she do that?

"What?"

"Umm, sir did you mess the bathroom up?" The lady looked at him.

"Bitch, why you telling my business."

"I'm sorry, I was.-" The cashier was extremely nervous.

"You were nothing. You think I wanted this chick to know I just shitted in there? Huh? Or that the toilet is clogged and probably won't work for a while? Tha fuck is wrong with you? Where's your manager? I think we need a discount or a free meal." I laughed so fucking hard I never realized the woman coming from the back until she spoke. The cashier handed me the food and tried to ignore him.

"How can I help you sir?" She stepped around the counter and I couldn't help but stare.

This woman was beautiful even in the tight ass brown uniform she wore. She had a caramel complexion, light brown eyes but not hazel and the way her hair bounced you could tell she went to a salon. Her ass was perfectly round in those pants and her titties sat up nice. There was a dimple on the right side of her cheek and the top retainer she wore still had her looking sexy.

"Oh damn. What happened in the bathroom?" She held her nose.

"I don't know." Fazza said with a straight face. She moved closer and her eyes grew wide.

"Bridget after that customer, print out an out of order sign for the men's bathroom. I'll have to get a plumber here ASAP." She closed the door and shook her head.

"I'm sorry about that. What seems to be the problem?" I caught her cleaning the top of the garbage can off with a rag. I was impressed she took pride in her job. Most women see men and forget they have one. They start flirting and pretending not to care if they get fired or not.

"Your cashier BRIDGET!" He said and stared at the poor girl ringing up another customer.

"Thought it would be funny to not only assume I'm the one who clogged y'all toilet but shouted it out in front of other customers." She looked over at the cashier who put her head down.

"Sir, I apologize on behalf of my employee. I will make sure to handle the situation once the customers leave."

"Good because she needs to be fired or suspended."

"Can I offer to comp your meal?" She was being patient as hell with Fazza who started eating it up.

"I think we need some sort of restitution." The lady looked at Fazza.

"Restitution?" There goes her patience.

"Does this facility look like we give out restitution? If you want your money back or a gift card, I can do that but you're bugging with restitution." She moved past him and slipped on a napkin. I caught her and oddly both of us stared at each other.

"Let me find out you made a love connection bro." The woman asked me to let her up.

"Thank you for catching me and as for you." She pointed to Fazza.

"I'm going to give you a gift card but do me a favor and don't come back." She gave him a fake smile and stepped behind the counter.

"Thank you very much and I won't. I like Starbucks anyway."

"That's good to know. Go there and see if you get the code for the bathroom or maybe get arrested by the cops."

"That's very petty of you."

"So was you mentioning a competitive store. Anyway, here you go and remember what I said about not returning."

"Fuck you." She stopped and turned around.

"What did you say?" She began walking in our direction.

"You heard me. I don't stutter." She snickered and tried to run up on him. I caught her mid swing. Had she connected with my brother, her and every person in here would've been dead for being witnesses. I literally had to drag her to the back kicking and yelling. Luckily the last customer left before it happened. A person was coming in but they had earphones on.

"Calm down Zia." I said after reading her name tag.

"Fuck him. How dare he speak to me like that?" She was pacing back and forth in the office.

"You ok?" She was shaking and her eyes were watery. I knew women get like that when they were mad and couldn't do what they wanted.

"I'm fine." She stopped moving and glanced around the office.

"Shit, I just got this store managers position and I'm about to lose it already to some fuck nigga."

"You're not gonna lose your position." She looked at me.

"How you know?"

"No one was here and unless the cashier tells, who's gonna mention it?" She stared at me.

"He crosses me as the type to go online and leave a nasty review."

"Nah, he petty but not that petty. Look, don't let him get you worked up. He's a dick sometimes and the angrier you get, the more buttons he's gonna press."

"Are you serious?"

"Very. Now you have a good day." She stopped me from walking and wrapped her arms around me.

"Thank you so much for keeping me from making a fool of myself. I can't afford to lose this job. I really appreciate it." She stepped back and both of us were in a trance. Outta nowhere she closed the door and threw her tongue down my throat. I can't front, shorty is a great kisser but we don't even know one another.

"Oh my God. I'm so sorry. I don't know what came over me."

"Relax ma. It's ok." I opened the door back up.

"Whatever man is receiving those kisses is very lucky."
She blushed and I had to grab myself because she damn sure
turned me on.

"I'll see you around." She nodded and I walked out.
Fazza was already in the car eating his donuts.

"Now that was a quick nut."

"Man, I ain't fuck her."

"You should've. She bad as hell." I glanced in the store
as we were pulling out and shorty was standing there smiling. I
was gonna blow my horn but I didn't wanna embarrass her.

Maybe one day we'll meet again. What am I saying? I
have a girl. She may be irking my nerves and, on her way out
but I didn't stop Zia from kissing me either. Does that mean
I'm over Riley? Only time will tell.

That man was way passed fine but I had no business kissing him. What the hell came over me, I couldn't even tell you. It could be my man hasn't fucked me in what eight or nine months. Or the fact I know he's cheating and every time I bring it up, he finds a way to make it like I'm crazy or bugging. Or maybe it's me wanting a one-night stand, just to get off. Lord knows the toys can only do so much.

It's not that my man Jordan isn't attractive because he's every woman's dream. He's tall, light skinned, had deep waves in his hair and he stayed in the gym. Everything he wore was expensive and it could be because he owned five gyms, a few convenient stores and a laundromat. I did inquire about him being an ex-drug dealer but his parents are fucking loaded, pushing that thought out the window.

I mean they had money over top of money due to them hitting the lottery for like three hundred million or some shit. Then they invested in business, stocks and other things. Not to mention, they gave their kids money and all of them did well with it.

Anyway, the reason we haven't had sex in a while isn't because of me at all. Jordan is the type of man who points out all your flaws, yet; forgets his own.

For instance, I'm not skinny at all and I have a small belly because I love to eat. My thighs are thick and my ass and titties are pretty much stacked. I'm not fat but definitely what men called slim thick. I'm about 5'6 and I weigh possibly 155 pounds. Unfortunately, when I get naked, my imperfections come to surface and he has no problem mentioning each and every one.

I have areas of cellulite around my thigh area, my stomach isn't that big but when I sit you can tell I have one. My arms aren't big at all but I do have the little swimmers under them. You know when you wave your hand and the upper part of your arm has that skin that waves too. Yea, that.

Jordan has told me on plenty of occasions that nothing's wrong with me but if that's the case, why doesn't he touch me? I mean, I can be butt ass naked in the bed and he'll fall asleep. If I put on a lingerie set from Victoria secrets he won't have an issue touching me. Is it because I'm covered up?

Or how about when I come out the shower in just a towel. I'll

take it off and he won't even look. And to make matters worse,

he'll see a woman on television and compliment everything

about her.

I don't know if he does it on purpose but mentally it's

fucking me up. It makes me feel like I'm not good enough. If

he wants those type of chicks then it's best for him to leave me

alone. And before anyone assumes I haven't, trust me I've tried

to leave him plenty of times and I'm sad to admit that

financially, I need him or should I say needed him. My mom

lives in the projects and I won't resort to going back there.

He paid my cell phone, light and cable bill but I refused

to allow him to pay my rent. I'll be without all that other shit

but no man will take pride in saying they pay that. He helps me

with food sometimes and gives me gas for my car.

I only have my high school diploma because I hated

school. Plus, the shit you learn in college to get your degree is

useless. The job you get is going to teach you their way so why

bother. And now minimum wage going up and people working

in fast food places are making just as much as people with

degrees. Hell, the promotion I just got to run this store pays me twenty dollars an hour. It may not be much to some but for me it's a hella lot. I can now pay my own bills, buy my own food and splurge on some of the stores in the mall.

Of course, I like nice things like most women and Jordan spends a lotta money on me but I'm fine with clothes from Express and Fashion Nova. The problem I have with him buying me clothes is that when we go out, he loves to pretend I'm something I'm not. Its mostly at functions his parents threw which only catered to older people.

On a few occasions he's even mentioned the things he does for me, which is why kissing that man only made me see things for what they were and that's, that I'm unhappy and need to move on and be by myself.

"Goodnight Bridget." I turned the lights off and locked up the store. One of the employees always stayed with me to close and I appreciated it. They'd get off at eight and stick around until ten or eleven when I was done. They didn't even get paid for it, which is why I never had a problem giving them extra hours or overtime.

"Night Zia and I forgot to ask. Did you get the guys number?" She started her car and came over to me.

"Girl you know I have a man." She sucked her teeth. Everyone has witnessed Jordan's conceited ass come in pretending he was better than the universe.

"I say if you won't leave him, at least have some fun on the side. We all know he is." She said and left me sitting in my car. I thought about what she said and maybe I will do just that. I mean, at least someone will touch me. This pussy drought is not what it is.

Instead of going home, I drove over to this house I've been looking at to buy. It was beautiful, and in an all-white area. Sad to say but sometimes they're the safest place to live, especially in Maryland.

It has three bedrooms, a master bathroom, a big kitchen, living and dining room and a decent size backyard. I tried to get my mom to move with me but she refuses to leave the hood. Talking about how would she get the latest gossip and see the hood rats fight. She was a trip but I loved her.

The realtor and I have been in here at least four times because I kept being picky. I loved it but Jordan kept saying it was too small and I should get something bigger. He resided in a huge mansion, where I'm ok in a small spot. I had fifty thousand dollars in my bank account no one knew of because I had been saving since I was a kid. I had another five in a savings account for emergency thanks to Jordan. Being he's so rich I should have more but he's a cheap fuck when it comes to handing out money. If he purchased it on his credit card, he looked at it as not actually giving you money. Yes, he was very anal about shit like that.

Anyway, with me being a first-time homebuyer I get a lot of credits. Now I'm waiting for the closing to arrive, to get my keys and be rid of that studio place I've been living in. Jordan, claimed to love that place. Yea right. We bump into one another all the time and when he pisses me off, the only place that had a door on it was the bathroom. Shit, the toilet seat hurts when you sit on it too long but I've done it long enough to be used to it. At least, I'll have quite a bit of doors to slam in his face and have alone time.

****

"Jordan." I called out his name when I got to his house. He lived closer to the neighborhood and since it was late I didn't feel like driving home.

"Jordan." He still didn't answer. I took my sneakers off and slowly walked all the steps to the bedroom. Like I said before, his house is huge because he loved showing off his wealth. I have no problem with someone being proud of the things they owned but he was always obnoxious, rude and ignorant about it.

I checked the bathroom because he takes late showers and he wasn't in there, I opened the bedroom door and shouldn't have been shocked but I was. I covered my mouth and stared as my man laid there getting his dick rode by some chick, as another one sat on his face. I was hurt beyond hurt and my heart was broken. He may be an ass but I did love him.

Just by looking at their bodies, either they stayed in the gym too or had a lotta work done. It only proved my point of not being what he wanted sexually. I stood there tryna decipher if I should say something or leave. I went with the latter and walked down the steps but not before snapping a picture with my phone because he'll deny it and leaving his house keys. I removed mine from his key ring, and left the same way I arrived, quietly. I picked my phone up and dialed the only person I knew would understand.

"Ma, what you doing?" I asked when she answered. It was around 11:30 which means she's most likely on the porch being nosy. Where she lived, everyone came out at night.

"Chilling. You coming over?"

"Yea." I said in a sad voice.

"What he do?"

"He cheated or should I say he's cheating right now."

"Honey you knew he was dipping out." I hate when people say I told you so. I assumed he was cheating but I never walked into like I did tonight. No other woman has ever contacted me about him so whether I assumed it or not, I never witnessed it like I did tonight.

"I'll be over in a few." I hung up and let the tears fall down my face. He may have mentally fucked me up but he was still my man. Not only was he having sex with those women, I heard him moaning as he ate the chicks' pussy, which means

he was enjoying himself. Say what you want but certain things

are for the main chick in my opinion. I guess everyone don't

think the same.

On the way over, I stopped at the diner and it was

crowded. Not tryna hear my mom's mouth at the moment, I

went inside and as luck would have it there was an empty table

in the back by the bathroom. Not that I wanted to be this close

to it but I needed alone time and this is fine. I sat down and the

waitress took my order.

"If you came for water why didn't you stay home?" I

looked up and it was the same guy from earlier. I used the back

of my hands to wipe my face.

"What are you doing here?" His facial expression

changed when he saw mine.

"My brother and I came to town for business and

decided to have something to eat before going out."

"Great. The other guy is here with you?" I scoffed up a

laugh.

"Don't be like that." He took a seat opposite of me.

"What's a beautiful woman like yourself sitting over here alone and crying?" He used his thumb to catch one of my lone tears.

"How can a man who has the perfect woman at home cheat? I'm not saying I'm the best woman in the world but I did everything for him; even pretended to be someone I'm not just to make him look good in front of everyone and he still steps out. What is it that women do wrong to make a man cheat?" He leaned back in his chair and stared at me for a few minutes. It actually made me uncomfortable.

"A man is only going to do what a woman allows." I looked at him.

"I'm not saying you did because we don't know one another but my mother always told me, a woman knows when her man steps out. She gets this feeling in her gut and she will try and push it away but it will still be there. The only way for the feeling to go away is to have solid proof and from the way you look, it's safe to assume you just found out."

"Is it that obvious." I accepted the water from the lady.

"A woman crying usually gives an indication that somethings wrong but you could've been upset over anything."

"I guess you're right." I sat the water on the table.

"What the fuck? Is he serious right now?" The guy turned around and both of us watched as Jordan and the two women strolled in like a happy couple and took a seat on the other side of the restaurant. This couldn't be my life, could it?

When shorty yelled out what the fuck, I turned to see the same guy we had a meeting with earlier. What are the damn odds of her being his woman? Now I understood why she said he tried to make her someone she wasn't in front of his family and friends. This man had a lotta money and you could tell she was beneath him just by the way he spoke during our conversation.

Now that I think of it, he had no photos in his office of her and to be honest, I thought him and the secretary had something going. They blatantly flirted in front of us and when we left, she damn near ran in the office.

Needless to say, the meeting didn't go as planned. Dude was way too cocky and had no idea about the drug world. He explained how his family came into the money but he never picked up, bagged or sold any type of drug. I would be stupid as hell to supply him. He's the type of guy who'll fuck up, snitch and disappear into witness protection. That's how doofy and dumb he was.

Now he had his main woman in here crying her eyes out about him and walks in with two women. They were pretty but not better looking than Zia. You could tell right off the bat, money paid for their bodies and hair. The clothes and shoes were expensive too but now a days chicks can get them from anywhere on a discount.

"What you gonna do?" I asked and she sat there.

"Nothing."

"Nothing? Zia, your man walked in here with two women and you're not going to do anything?"

"I'm gonna show you why. Watch this?" She stood and made her way over to him.

"Yo, ain't that shorty from Dunkin Donuts?" Fazza said when I sat back at the table. The other two guys looked up.

"Yea and that's her man."

"Corny dude?"

"Yup. He walked in with those two chicks and I asked her what she's gonna do and she told me to watch." All of us turned to look. He didn't sit far from us and a lotta people left so we could hear their entire conversation.

"Jordan, what's this?" She pointed to the two women. His eyes got big as hell.

"Who are you?"

"Jordan, I'm talking to you." She totally ignored the chick.

"Jordan, I know you aren't messing with someone who works at Dunkin Donuts." She still had her uniform on and I could tell she was uncomfortable with the way she said it.

"And what's wrong with where I work?"

"My man has too much class to be with someone below him."

"Your man?"

"Oh shit yo. How he got three girlfriends?" My brother asked being funny.

"You know what Jordan. I can't do this no more." Her voice started cracking, which means she was about to break.

"Hold on Zia." He attempted to get up. She turned and walked in our direction.

"You know her?" One of the chicks asked.

"That's why I didn't say anything. He doesn't admit to being with me in front of people." She grabbed her purse, and phone and stormed out. I thought about going after her but he did.

"She gonna take him back." My brother said and we all got up to go. We were on our way to a strip club.

"Let's go see some ass and titties shake." Kelly said. He's addicted to those damn places.

As we walked out, I noticed he had her leaned on the car as he stood in front of her. Shorty's face was turned up and we could hear him apologizing over and over. I shook my head and got in my car.

"That nigga must have a golden dick because he damn sure back in her good graces." Kelly said and we all looked. He had his face in her neck. I laughed because she rolled her eyes. Once he removed his face, she opened her car door, closed it and peeled out.

"I need to make a stop." Kelly's cousin, Steph said who was with us. He's the one we always linked up with when we came down.

"A'ight. But hurry up." We pulled up to the projects and got out. Usually we stay in the car but Fazza wanted to smoke and I hate my car having that smell. It only gave cops a reason to search and regardless of nothing being in the car, I don't want them searching my shit.

"Ima be quick. This woman said her daughter needed to smoke some trees. I'm only stopping by because she offered to pay me two hundred dollars."

"Damn, her daughter must be tryna get fucked up."

"This woman usually spends more than that." He smiled and started to walk towards the person's house.

"Word?" Fazza questioned.

"Yea she cool as hell. We even have smoke parties in her spot.

"Well shit, why we standing out here? Let's go inside and get it popping. She got drinks?"

"Probably."

We made our way to the door and some older woman opened the screen. For her to be older she was pretty and had a nice body. You could tell she smoked a lot by how brown her lips were. She told us to come in and shockingly, her crib was nice as hell. She had a flat screen on the wall, her furniture looked expensive and her house was spotless. That's unusual for people living in the hood.

"Y'all can have a seat." She closed the door.

"Z, we got company so don't come out with no clothes on." We all looked in her direction.

"What? I taught her not to be ashamed of her body so when she's here, it's whatever."

"Damn. You shouldn't have said anything." Kelly's perverted ass was always looking for ass.

"Anyway. Her man got caught cheating and she's staying here for a while." She offered up the information probably to let us know the reason for all the weed.

"Damn!"

"I told her to leave his ass alone." She took out some blunt paper and passed Kelly's cousin the money.

"Sometimes women have to see things for themselves." I told her and asked to use the bathroom once the bedroom door shut.

She pointed and told me to excuse all the women items inside. I laughed at the amount of lotions, soaps and sprays that lined the shelf inside. It didn't bother me because Riley did the same shit at our house, which reminds me to call her back.

After I finished and washed my hands, I picked my cell up and opened the door only to run straight into Zia. Both of us were shocked and I could hear Riley yelling through the phone. I told her I'd call her back and stared at shorty who only had a towel on.

"Didn't your mom say y'all had company?" She shifted her weight to the side and put her hands on her hips.

"And? I didn't expect them to use our bathroom."

"Yea well. I had to go." We both stood there and I couldn't help but lick my lips. She was thick in all the right places and the leftover water dripping from her hair only turned me on more. She tucked some of it behind her ear and put her head down.

"I'm not down there." I made her look at me.

"Ummmm, let me put some clothes on."

"Nah, you look good this way." She blushed again.

"Do you know I have no clue what your name is?" I chuckled and moved closer.

"It's Mazza and at this point, does it really matter?" I slid my hand through her tangled hair and tilted her head back.

"I shouldn't be doing this but I can't stop thinking about that kiss."

"Me neither." She wrapped her arms around my neck and the two of us stood there engaging in inappropriate behavior. We both had someone, well I did and she's in a complicated situation.

"Mmmm hmmm. It's nice to see you moving on." Her mom leaned on the wall smoking.

"Oh shit." Zia shouted because her towel opened.

"Don't be ashamed. I like what I see." I rewrapped the towel and watched her run in the room.

"I don't know you but if you have a situation leave my daughter alone. She's been with that loser for a few years and she doesn't need another heartbreak."

"I respect it and you're right. I'm in a relationship and I've never cheated on her but something about Zia is drawing

88

me in. It's probably best for me to go. Tell her I apologize for overstepping." I went in the living room and told the guys to come on. If not, I'm not sure Zia and I wouldn't be naked and fucking up some headboards.

"Don't do it Z." My mom opened the door to my old bedroom. After the shit with Jordan I drove straight here.

He had the nerve to come out the restaurant to tell me the women were just friends and he doesn't know why the woman said that. To make matters worse, he started kissing on my neck in front of the Mazza guy on purpose. I pushed him off, showed him the photo in my phone of him having sex with the two chicks and pulled off. I can still see the dumb look on his face when he saw it.

Then, I get here and jump straight in the shower, go in my room to grab some clothes and run into the Mazza guy again. It has to be some fate or coincidence that we ran into one another three times in one night. The kiss we shared here was more explosive than the one in Dunkin Donuts. I don't know what's going on but I damn sure liked it.

"Don't do what ma?" I asked and got in the bed. I heard the front door close which mean the guys left. I picked the opened blunt wrapper up off the nightstand and started rolling it. Yea, I smoke every now and then. It helps me relax when I'm going through things.

My mom buys all my weed because she said niggas be tryna hustle people. I think she's low key sleeping with the dude who sells it to her. They don't want no one to know because he's younger but shit she's forty-four and he's thirty-three. That ain't bad to me but my lips are sealed.

"Z, that man is sexy as hell and I can see how attractive you are to one another."

"Ma, we only kissed in the spur of the moment."

"Exactly. What if I didn't stop y'all and you went in the room? Can you honestly say nothing would've happened?" I licked the blunt and picked up the lighter.

"No I can't and who cares?" She sat on my bed.

"He has a girl." The moment she said it, I was devastated. Not because it was love at first sight or anything like that but because I already had him as my boyfriend in my head. I laughed at myself and passed my mom the blunt.

"Why am I not surprised?"

"He said to tell you, he apologizes for overstepping."

"At least he has some home training."

"True." She took her shoes off and hopped on the other side of the bed. Her phone kept ringing.

"Ma, he can come over."

"It's ok. My baby is here. He knows what time it is." I laughed and the two of us sat up until early morning watching TV and smoking. I miss these days with her.

"We'll get your things later." She said. I told her I'd be staying here until the closing on my new house. I knew Jordan wouldn't come here because he hates the projects. He's too good to step foot on the sidewalk. At least, I don't have to deal with his lying ass again.

****

"You sure this is trash?" Steph asked. He's the guy my mom is secretly seeing. She had him and two other guys come help me get my things. I told her I could do it but she didn't want Jordan coming over and tryna talk me outta moving.

"Yea, everything can go as far as furniture. The only things I'm taking are my clothes and important papers."

"A'ight." They started bringing the stuff to the curb. There's nothing wrong with my furniture and it's actually in pretty good shape. However, if I'm moving into a new house you can bet I'm getting new furniture.

Two hours later we had finally finished and we were beat. The place was cleaned out and the last thing I had to do was give the landlord back the key. I wasn't worried about a security deposit because I only gave him five hundred. This studio had a lot of good memories with Jordan in the beginning but ended off with a lotta bad ones.

"What's going on Zia and why did you call me over here?" Jordan asked scanning the studio apartment.

"Can y'all give us a minute?"

"Just a minute because we got shit to do." My mom said and rolled her eyes. She couldn't stand him and the feeling is mutual. I don't know how many times she cursed him out or the amount of bitches he called her.

I went in the closet and pulled out the two big totes of his things. There were clothes, a couple pair of sneakers and a few suits from the nights he stayed here. I could see the confusion on his face but this needed to be done. I moved closer to him, kissed his cheek and headed towards the door.

"What's going on Zia?"

"I'm moving in with my mom until I close on the house and we are over." He ran over to me and gripped the top of my arm so tight, I know my circulation stopped.

"Get off of me." I tried to break free.

"You listen here bitch."

"Bitch?" That's the second time in two days I've been disrespected.

"That's right, I said it. You're not going no fucking where."

"Jordan, if I tell you to let me go again, I'm gonna scream."

"And I'm gonna hit you so fucking hard, all your teeth will hit the ground." I don't know what got into him but this isn't the arrogant, corny, stuck up Jordan I knew. This man was someone else and I'm glad to get away from him.

"Now you listen and listen well." He pushed me hard against the wall. My tailbone hit the hinge of the door. It felt like someone kicked me in the back.

"You can stay with your ghetto ass mother for now but we're not over and won't ever be." I stared at him.

"Jordan what's wrong with you? You're sleeping with other women, you talk down on me, we haven't even had sex in almost a year. Why are you doing this?" I was rubbing my tailbone because it hurt bad as hell.

"Because I've been paying these bills."

"Please. The damn cell phone, cable and lights."

"Doesn't matter. Your ass would've been living in the dark. Now like I said." He let my arm go and pulled my ponytail.

"If you even think about leaving me, I'll make sure that house deal falls through and that little bit of money you think you're hiding will be removed from your bank account." My mouth fell open.

"Yea I know about all of it. I suggest you get it together. Now I'm gonna give you a week or two to get passed this attitude but I expect you by my side at the grand opening of the new gym in Delaware."

"Jordan I'm not..." He yanked my hair harder.

"You don't have a fucking choice." He planted a rough kiss on my lips, let go of my hair and I hit the floor. He opened the front door and looked back at me.

"Don't make me come looking for you." He slammed the door. What in the hell am I gonna do now?

"Are you ok?" My mom walked in as I got off the floor.

"Yea." I went in the kitchen to see if there was any ice left.

"Why are you limping? Did he put his hands on you?"

"No ma. He's mad I don't wanna be with him. He tried to kiss me and I backed into the door." She gave me a crazy look. Its like she knew I was lying and to be honest, I have no idea why I didn't tell her the truth. Maybe its because I might take him back and didn't want to be judged by more than him cheating on me. Who knows? Whatever the case, I needed some ice and some sort of pain pill to help alleviate this discomfort in my back.

Me and my mom walked out together after handing the key to the landlord. I opened the passenger side door and tried to sit but like I said, it was painful. Steph noticed and told my mom to take me to the hospital. She accused Jordan of being the reason for my back and even told the people at the hospital my ex is most likely the reason for it. They gave me a sad look that only pissed me off.

I'm sure they've seen women in domestic abuse relationships on a regular but I'm not one of them. Crazy as it may seem, this is the only time Jordan has every laid a hand on me. Mentally he was all around an asshole but physically, this has never happened. Thankfully, I'll be staying far away from him as possible.

"Ok, Mrs. Robinson, you have a bruised tailbone." The doctor said and my mom gave me a nasty look.

"The x-rays didn't show any other damage so I'm going to send you home and prescribe you some pain medication. Its going to take a few weeks for you to feel better so I wrote you a note for work in case you need it." He said as I felt myself drifting in and out of sleep. The medication they gave me through the IV worked fast as hell.

"Take one of these three times a day for pain and make sure you see your regular doctor to follow up." I nodded and tried my best to help my mom get me dressed. Once we got the discharge papers, the nurse wheeled me to the car. Getting up and down was hella painful.

"Thank you." I slurred speaking to the nurse. She smiled and closed the car door. I don't remember how I got in the house but I do know, my ass was knocked out once my head hit the pillow.

"Why are you stressing yourself Riley? You know he's not a cheater." Evelyn said as we sat in her office having lunch.

"I know but ever since he came back from Maryland two weeks ago, he's been different."

"Different how?" I thought about the night he returned.

The day before he was supposed to come home I called him and he didn't answer. He called me back and I heard a female in the background. I yelled out who was she and he hung up saying he'd call me back. That call didn't come until the next day. When I asked who she was, he said they were at a strip club. I would've believed him, had it not been quiet in the background. We all know the music is always blasting in clubs and you can still hear it in the bathroom and outside.

Anyway, he came home two days later talking about they stayed longer to check out their workers and some other shit. That's fine but the kicker was when I attempted to have sex with him. He claimed to be tired and not want it. That's very unusual for a man who gives it to me whenever, wherever. I even tried to give him head and he refused that too. I may be

99

bugging but it felt like another woman was occupying his brain but who and how? I check his phone records and no new number pops up. He doesn't do any social media so I can't check there and he still has the same routine. Could I be bugging?

"I don't know Evelyn but I feel it in my gut."

"Do you think you're paranoid because of the shit you're doing?" I sucked my teeth. I wasn't cheating per say. However, I did meet a guy who had money. The two of us have been texting a lot as of lately and he's coming into town this weekend.

"I haven't done anything with the guy." Evelyn gave me the side eye.

"Texting, sending nude photos, talking on the phone and even entertaining another man is cheating. It may not be physical but the aspects of being with another man is there. All you have to do is sleep with him and if I know you, that's exactly what you'll be doing this weekend."

"Evelyn he's so sweet, attentive, understanding and makes me cum so hard during phone sex it's ridiculous." I think the thrill of me being in a relationship makes it more fun. I don't know why, it just does.

"I hear you but I'm gonna say this and we don't ever have to discuss it again." I put the fork to my salad down.

"Mazza has done nothing wrong thus far. If you don't wanna be with him, I suggest you let him know because we both know how he'll react if he finds out you dipped out." I sat there listening to her logic. It went in one ear and out the other.

"You don't have to listen but are you ready to lose everything for a man you don't know? Or are you ready to die behind a man who'll most likely forget you once he doesn't hear from you?" I didn't say anything.

"Think Riley. I know it's fun right now but is it worth it?"

"I guess you're right. What if I only sleep with him once?" She laughed.

"Riley you're gonna do what you want. I'm just trying to be the voice of reason. I don't wanna lose my best friend."

Again, she had me thinking. I worked hard to keep Mazza away from the trifling whores running the streets. Am I ready to lose him? Can I deal with him spending time with a new woman or women? I damn sure don't want another bitch sampling his dick. *Decisions, Decisions.*

****

"Excuse me." The woman with her kids said. She bumped into me as we ran into the store to get out the rain.

"Oh it's you." I said and rolled my eyes. Nothing about the woman changed. Shit, she appeared to be doing better than when we previously met six years ago. Her hair was laid, nails done, clothes looked expensive and the kids were well kept too.

"Long time no see, hidden trash."

"What the hell is hidden trash and I'm sure you didn't miss me."

"You're right I didn't and hidden trash is what you are or should I say were to Shakim." I laughed at her jealousy.

"I highly doubt that."

"No it's what you were." She smirked.

"How you figure?"

"Because he kept you locked away in that house like a prisoner, while he and I roamed the streets freely with our children. Everyone knew about us but no one knew you existed. And before you ask, yes I knew about you." She looked me up and down.

"The stupid virgin who allowed a man to beat her ass, alienate you from your family, fucked you any way he wanted and made you engage in threesomes. You did any and everything for a man who used you."

"Used me?"

"Yup. Kids go over there." She pointed to an area with chairs inside the mall.

"He made you do dope drops for him, correct?" I didn't answer and let her continue.

"Had you sticking drugs in your pussy too, right? Or what about the time he made you fuck a man in front of him as he slept with two women in the opposite bed. What kind of man who's in love with a woman would allow her to please anyone but him?"

The shit she brought up from the past hit a nerve. How did she know all those things and was Shakim using me? He did have me doing weird stuff but it's because he didn't trust anyone else. Did he alienate me from my family and the world to showcase her? We went on vacations and things like that so how could he not love me. But then again, no one knew about that either because we'd be alone. I went shopping and even had a car. Granted, he sent someone with me and I couldn't be out longer than two hours. Damn, was I that blind to not notice?

"If you knew that why'd you stick around? What does that say about you?" I tried to appear unbothered.

"Honey, I left him alone months before he passed after finding out. Why you think he started whooping your ass? You were the cause of me leaving. I'm surprised he didn't kill you." I went to walk away because I was done listening.

"Honey, don't be upset. It happens all the time to young bitches who wanna be grown. They get caught up with a guy who uses, abuses and tosses them away. Then wanna cry and boo hoo because a real woman stepped in. But let's be clear on

104

one thing before you walk away and cry in the car." She moved closer and we were now face to face.

"I know in my heart you had something to do with his death and when I find out the truth, my cousin Mazza won't be able to save you."

"Cousin?" I questioned.

"Yes, my cousin." She smirked as if the shit she just told me was amusing.

"He never told me you were related?"

"And I never told him you were with Shakim either."

"I don't believe you. Why haven't we met at family functions?"

"I never came if you were going to be there because I hated you and still do. I also knew from my aunt how much he loves you and didn't wanna hurt him. Shit, you and I both know if Mazza knew you were with Shakim, he'd never give you the time of day."

"Whatever."

"Say what you what but who you think got the twins acquainted with Shakim? Why do you think he took them under his wing and molded them to take over when he stepped down?" She laughed.

"That young pussy may have been good for the moment to him but he knew where home was. He knew the best place on earth for his dick was inside me." She pointed to her two kids and blew me a kiss.

"Fuck you bitch."

"Tsk. Tsk. Tsk." She waved her index finger.

"I wouldn't be disrespectful to the woman who's gonna take your life. It might have an impact on how I torture you."

"Torture me?"

"Remember, the twins are my cousin and I've seen and learned a lot from them."

"Mazza would never allow it."

"If it comes out that you took away his mentor, I doubt he'll care and I pray he doesn't get you before me. Tootles." She winked and stepped off. I had to find a way to get rid of her. If she or the twins found out what really happened with Shakim, I can kiss my life goodbye.

Watching that stupid bitch walk away only fueled the fire in me towards her. I literally wanted to snatch her up by the hair and beat the living daylights outta her. However, my kids are here and I try my hardest not to ever let them see me outta character. Granted, they may have seen an argument here or there but never witnessed me fighting anyone.

I grabbed my kids hands and walked into the sneaker store. The whole time all I could think about was making sure the bitch got exactly what she deserved. Shakim's death may have been ruled an accident but I know deep down she had something to do with it. I don't care how innocent she plays. The bitch is scandalous and trifling. Once I expose her, I'm hoping my cousin lets me take her life.

See, I knew all about Riley prior to Shakim's death. I found out because one day he and I were out shopping and he asked me to hold his phone while he used the bathroom. I never thought anything of it because if he were cheating, no one ever approached me and it never crossed my doorstep.

Anyway, Riley text and asked when he was coming home? Now, I'm confused as hell because to my knowledge, he didn't have any other houses. Shit, the one I resided in was huge. Nonetheless, I scrolled through more messages and that's when I realized he had another woman. I waited until we got home to confront him and unfortunately that's when it all came out.

I was hurt to find out he had her in a nice house as well, took her on a few vacations. When we had the fallen out over it, he admitted she was some young girl he was having fun with. He explained all the dumb shit he had her doing too. I could tell by her facial expressions that she was hurt and shocked he filled me in on as much as he did. Little did she know, I'm probably the exact reason she began to get her ass beat even more than what he'd already done.

I ended up leaving him because I refused to be with a man who had a side chick portraying the life as if she were his woman. I mean he had her living nice and I found that out after kicking her out. I admit she had good taste in clothes and shoes but I handed it all over to the goodwill. The furniture, cars and everything else is gone too. I even sold the house. Ain't no way in hell I'd live in it.

Now she's living with my cousin and he's clueless about who she really is. No one knew but me and that's because Shakim never, ever brought her anywhere for people to see. As far as I know, he also made her stay locked in the room if he had company there. *Crazy, I know.*

I wanted to tell Mazza the moment I found out they were together but my mom told me how much he loved her. Sad to say, once Shawn informs me of the truth, nothing is going to stop me from telling my cousin and killing her. Say what you want but the bitch is sneaky, trifling and needs to pay for her part in my kids' father death.

"Mommy, can we get something to eat?" My daughter asked just as my phone rang. It was a message from the lead detective in Shakim's case. He too believed foul play was involved and even though the state closed the case, he remained on it.

Shawn: *Hey babe. Am I coming over tonight?"*

Me: *Yes. I can't wait to see you.* Oh yea. Did I forget to mention he and I were together?

It didn't happen right away but after spending countless nights alone with each other, it just happened. I don't mean I slid on the dick by accident or anything like that but neither of us expected anything to transpire. We've only been involved for the last three years and no one knows what he does. The reason I haven't told them is because let's be real. How many people fuck with the cops? Especially; when you have cousins, who run everything.

Anyway, his family loved me and my kids. I've been at every BBQ, and whatever event or function they've thrown. It took me a minute to be ok with attending anything because I had to be sure the two of us would work.

He doesn't have any baby mamas; no disgruntled ex's and I had the key to both his houses and two cars. It's not to say he isn't cheating because these days you never know but he hasn't given me any reason to believe he's dipping out.

"Yes. Let's go to the food court." I paid for their

sneakers, responded to his text and continued thinking of all

the ways I'm gonna torture Riley.

"Just go see her bro." Fazza said speaking of Zia. Ever since we left Maryland, I couldn't get her off my mind. I thought about her constantly and the shit was interfering with Riley and my relationship.

The day I came home my girl tried to sleep with me but the moment she kissed me, all I saw was Z. She wanted to fuck and go down on me and still, Z was the only woman I saw. It's crazy because we ran into one another three times in one day, kissed twice and didn't even have long conversations. Yet; the need to see and speak to her plagued me every day.

"Man, I don't know if she's back with dude or what." That bothered me too. Zia was way to pretty and smart to fuck with a nigga like Jordan. His entire demeanor screamed arrogant, which is why we couldn't fuck with him. A man like him will make a motherfucker kill him because he'll fuck shit up, pretending to be something he's not.

"You won't know until you see her."

"Nah, I'm good. Riley is still my girl and.-" He sucked his teeth.

I knew he hated her and so did some of my family members. Hell, Tionne who is one of my favorite cousins won't even attend family functions because of Riley and to this day she won't tell me why. I have to see her and the kids when I'm alone.

I know she misses Shakim and we all do, which is why I try and visits as much as possible. Fazza takes the kids out a lot and I've been to the sports activities they're in too. I do wish she told me the reason why. When I ask my girl, she claims not to even know who's she is so I left it alone. I guess one day she'll tell me the real reason.

"I've been thinking about leaving Riley." He stared at me as we stepped out the car.

"Not because of Z but she's been moving funny lately."

"What you mean?" We walked in the building and headed straight to my office.

"I can't put my finger on it but I think she's cheating or about to." After putting our things down, we left and made our way to another room.

"Say word?"

"I know right. The way she stalks me and shit is crazy, yet she may be doing the exact thing she's accusing me of." We walked in and picked up the bow and arrow. The people inside had a look of terror on their faces, as they should. I pulled the arrow back and pointed it in the direction of my target.

"You know it's gonna be a problem getting rid of her if you do." I aimed the pointer at the spot I wanted to hit first, made sure it was accurate and let go.

"NOOOOOO!" I heard and watched as the arrow pierced through his heart.

"One down, four to go." I picked up another arrow and so did Fazza.

"Bro, you get two. I get two. Don't get greedy because you going through something." I laughed because it's been plenty of times we had to get rid of people and I killed them all just to have a bigger body count.

Like I explained earlier, my goal is to never kill people who fucked us over because they wouldn't live to tell what happened or show others not to do it. However, there are times

114

such as these where living without certain limbs is no longer an option.

These five individuals are here because they thought stealing from us is ok. Its different when you take from others but when you deliberately dip into our funds, it becomes a serious problem.

Each one worked in separate spots yet; were all in cahoots together. The crazy thing is, none of them thought they'd get caught. Its not like they took hundreds of thousands but taking a dollar was too much when it came to our money. And if you'll steal once, you'll steal again.

"Please don't." The woman that Fazza aimed his arrow at cried out. It fell on deaf ears as he let go. It went straight through her stomach. He loved to see them suffer before dying, which she's doing right now.

"My turn and this time I'm going for the neck." The last three people tried to put their chins down but it didn't help. The way they were held up against the wall with their body spread out and chained up, it was no use.

"Yo, that shot was perfect." I smiled at my work because it was. The arrow landed directly in the middle of the guys neck where his Adam's apple is.

"Fuck this. I'm going for the forehead."

"Nigga really?"

"Hell yea. These arrows have titanium tips. You and I both know it can go through the skull." I shook my head and sure enough it went through.

"Its one left. I got tails." I said and pulled a quarter out my jeans.

"I got the last one." We turned around and Tionne came strolling in, dressed in black.

"Where the hell you come from?"

"You don't wanna know. Trust me." The way she looked had me wondering. I left it alone and both of us watched as she shot the last person straight through their nose. Don't ask why we picked weird spots, we just do. All of us dropped the bow and arrows and went upstairs to talk.

If you're wondering where we are, it's a business we call CHAMBERS PLACE. Chambers is our last name which makes sense to call it that. And it's also where we brought people who fucked us over and either tortured or killed them. We do have a smaller warehouse where we do some small things such as, cut limbs off and things like that but we did a lot more here.

When you walk in, it looks like a regular business with people working in an office like atmosphere. They were doing work for us as far as the legal businesses we had and there were a lot. You had a conference room, staff room and all other amenities business held.

However, there was a secret elevator that camouflaged with the walls, located in both me and Fazza's office. If you walked in you'd never know it was there. The two of us are the only ones with the code. Very few knew of this place and we wanted to keep it this way.

Tionne got the passcode after Shakim died because we were teaching her to be safe. Niggas would try and come for her after his death and attempt to take everything from her and trust me; they've tried. I can't even begin to explain how many people lost their lives being stupid.

Anyway, the elevator went deep into the ground and even stepping off, all you'd see was dirt and rock. There was a long walkway that led to another hall. You had to touch a certain rock for it to lift up and inside we had all types of shit. The entire set up was off some TV shows but it was well worth it to keep the cops off our trail.

The room held torture chairs, guns, bow and arrows as you already know, and explosives. There's also an incinerator where we burned everything as well as that solution to clear away all blood. You can never be too careful.

I know it all sounds crazy but when you have two people who learned the tricks and trades from a maniac, you have no idea the things we come up with or do. A sane person would lose their mind just witnessing the room.

"What's up Tionne?" Fazza sat on the edge of my desk looking at her.

"Nothing. I just came by to see if the two of you were going to the grand opening of the new gym tomorrow."

"Why the hell we need to go there?"

"Because I wanna see it. Pleaseeeee."

"Tionne you don't need a gym." I told her. My cousin was in great shape. She had to be running behind the kids.

"Alright fine. I wanna join because the old one is shutting down. Evidently, the owner thinks this new one is going to put him outta business so he started telling us to look elsewhere." She plopped down in one of the chairs.

"Why didn't you just say that? I ain't doing shit, I'll go." Fazza looked at me.

"What?"

"I thought we were taking a ride out to Maryland." He said, still tryna convince me to see Zia. He wanted me away from Riley ASAP.

"Bye Faz. Go check on your girl."

"His girl?" Tionne stared at him.

"She ain't my girl until I test out the pussy."

"Really?" Tionne turned her face up. I hit the switch for my computer and ignored them. Those two can go at it for hours. At least, I'll get some work done.

✳✳✳✳✳✳✳✳✳✳✳✳✳✳

"Hey baby." Riley called out when I stepped in the house.

"Hey." I placed my keys on the table and walked up behind her. I loved my girl's body and the way her jeans had her ass sitting, I was definitely ready to fuck.

"I missed you." She turned and put her arms around my neck. I couldn't help but wonder where's she's been because whoever cologne it was, lingered.

"Where you been?" She dropped her arms and headed straight to the steps.

"Shopping." I noticed the few bags which is off for her. Riley always had a shit load of stuff and made me carry them in.

"Shopping huh. What you about to do?"

"Ugh. Take a shower." The hesitation in her voice confirmed she did something she had no business.

"You wanna join me?" She smiled.

"Nah. I'll be back." I picked my keys back up.

"Ok." Yea she doing something. It's never been a time Riley didn't complain if I came in and left right away. Ima find out what it is and soon.

"Hey. I didn't know you were coming over." I said to Fazza. I stepped out the shower and he was leaning on the wall smiling. I'm not sure if he were happy to see me or happy he finally saw me naked.

"This is my other house."

"It's is huh?" I grabbed the towel to dry off.

"Yup."

"That's news to me." I wrapped the towel and walked past only to be swung around. My back was against his chest and I could feel him becoming hard.

"Don't fucking move." He used both hands to unwrap my towel and let it hit the floor. I wanted to speak, but the way he took his time caressing both of my breasts and stimulating any and all sexual desires I had in my body, I couldn't speak a word.

"You like this?" He kissed my neck and used two of his fingers to roll over my nub that was bulging out of his lid.

"Yessssss." My head fell back on his shoulder.

"Tell me when you're ready." He circled faster.

122

"I'm ready. Shit, I'm fucking ready." It's been so long, I wanted to deliver exactly what he asked for.

"Go for it ma." He pressed down on my clit and my essence shot right outta my body. He had to catch me from falling.

"Damn, you needed that." He used his hand to push me down towards my ankles, bent down and sucked my pussy so damn good I think he absorbed every bit of fluid I had. When I assumed he was done and tried to get up, his finger delved in my asshole slowly. It hurt a little and felt good at the same time. My body began to shudder and my heart was racing.

Before I could enjoy that feeling, he latched back onto my pussy and drove me insane. I was grabbing the rug, yelling and trying my best to get away from his tongue. He had such a firm grip on me, I couldn't and by the time he finished giving me back to back orgasms, I laid my ass right on the floor.

I heard him laughing as he stood to unbutton his jeans. Again, my heart started to race because this is the moment I've been waiting for. I knew he was working with something, yet I still forbid myself from turning around to see. I wanted to be surprised. Plus, I may change my mind if I laid eyes on it first.

He lifted me up, carried me to the bed and went down on me again. My clit was super sensitive and he knew it because he kept playing. He'd suck, stop, then suck again and use his fingers. After bringing another one out I felt him rubbing the tip up and down my lower lips.

"This pussy better be as good as it tastes or we're done." I sucked my teeth. Here we are about to engage in what I hope is banging ass sex and he opens his mouth.

"This dick better be worth it or we're done." He smiled and spread my legs open further than they already were.

"Oh it is." I didn't respond as he inched his huge, thick and long dick inside. Usually I'm good on big dick dudes because it hurts too much but the way he took his time, made me relax and enjoy it.

"Fazza." I dug my nails in his biceps as he continued sliding in and out slow.

"Yea Ty." He was staring down at himself.

"I love you." He looked up and smiled. I've known for a while and was afraid to mention it.

"I know." I'm not gonna lie. I half expected him to say the same thing but he didn't. We've known each other almost five months and just because I fell hard doesn't mean he had to.

"Get on top." He pulled out, laid on his back and assisted me with guiding myself down.

"Shittttt." I moaned out when I felt the tip almost in my stomach. Or maybe it was in there. Whatever the case, he was deep as hell.

"You got this Ty." He placed his hands behind his head and enjoyed the show.

"Slow down ma. You're gonna make me cum." I was now riding him cowgirl style on my feet about to release for the second time.

"I will in a sec. Baby, I'm cumming again." He sat up, grabbed my breasts from behind and his teeth latched onto my back. He wasn't biting and the feeling was different and stimulating. It's like my body became hotter and my pussy became wetter, knowing how much he was enjoying it.

"You feel so got damn good Ty. Don't stop. Shit don't stop." I went faster as he smacked my ass a few times.

"Oh fuck girl." He squeezed my ass cheeks and both of us moaned out in ecstasy. I fell face forward on the bed and he fell back. You could hear both of us breathing heavy. I can't even tell you what happened next because I fell the fuck to sleep. I have never in my life, came so much or had a man do me that good.

****

"I'll be there soon." I opened my eyes when I heard Fazza on the phone.

"You up?"

"Yea."

"Good. I need a nut before I go." I threw the covers back on my head.

"You better give me some or I'll be forced to go..." he tried to say and I popped him in the mouth.

"You're mine from now on Fazza. If I hear or even think you're out there cheating on me, I swear to God.-" He snatched me out the bed.

126

"You swear what and who said I'm yours?"

"I did and I'm cutting your dick off while you sleep. You know I'll do it." I folded my arms.

"Damn, I strung you out last night huh?" I pushed him on the bed, got on my knees and with morning breath and all gave him the sloppiest and nastiest head ever.

"Oh shit. Oh shit. Ty, I'm about to. Oh fuckkkkkkkk." He grabbed my head and pumped his seeds in my mouth. I let my fingers play under his balls until he released everything he had. I stood up and stared at him lying on the bed with his eyes covered by his arm.

"Now unless you want another nigga tasting this good ass pussy you couldn't pull yourself away from eating or fucking; I suggest. No, I recommend you do your best at staying faithful. K." I patted his legs and left him staring at me walk in the bathroom.

I turned the shower on and went to the sink to brush my teeth and wash my face first. I gargled with mouthwash and just as I was about to step in the shower, he yanked me out and threw me against the wall. His dick twitched standing in front of me.

"Don't ever threaten me."

"Then don't make me." He made me look at him.

"I love you too Ty and if I even think you're out there entertaining a nigga in any way, I'll kill you." He placed a kiss on my lips and stepped in the shower.

The way he said it sent chills down my spine and not in a good way. We know men say that shit all the time but something about the tone of his voice had me scared for my life. Maybe I should leave him alone. But how can I, now that we both confessed our feelings. Let alone the mind-blowing sex.

"Get in here Ty." He pulled back the shower curtain and suds flowed down his body. I stepped in and stared at him.

"I'm gonna get you pregnant and if you get rid of it, take a plan b or miscarry, even by accident, I'm gonna take your mother's life." He had his hand around my throat.

"Fazza."

"This is what you wanted Ty." He had facing the wall.

"I…"

"You wanted all of me, right? Well you got me and you got my heart. Fuck with it and the consequences are deadly." He put both of my hands on the shower wall, opened my legs and entered with so much force I screamed out.

"Take all of it Ty."

"Fazza." I couldn't speak because the euphoria overtook my entire body. Here I am scared to death listening to his threats, yet; allowing him to do unimaginable things to my body.

"No other man better touch you. Do you hear me?" His lips were by my ear.

"Yessssss."

"Turn around." I tried to catch my breath and couldn't because he had me against the wall plunging deeper inside me.

"I want you and only you to carry my offspring's."

"Why me? Ahhh shit." I dug my nails in the top of his shoulders.

"Because you're the only women I've ever met worthy enough to do it. Fuckkkk, I'm cumming." He held me there and the two of us came together.

"Look at me." I managed to get my head up because all I wanted to do was sleep.

"I don't know when it happened but I am in love with you too. Don't do anything to make me regret it."

"I won't and the same goes for you." He nodded and we started kissing each other feverishly. I don't know what I just got myself into but as of right now, I don't even care.

"What time you get off?" I asked Ty. We were in front

of the hospital. We've been together everyday since we

admitted to loving each other and that was almost a month ago.

I can't lie; she was like a breath of fresh air to me.

If I had a bad day, she'd be right there to talk about it.

If I wanted sex, she never complained and sometimes initiated

it herself. There was always a home cooked meal for me;

regardless if she had to work late night or not. When I tell you

Ty is wife material, trust me she is.

"I work overnight. 7-7."

"I don't like that shit Ty. Who's your manager?" She

started laughing.

"Baby, I used to do it all the time. Now I only have to

once a month. When they hire more nurses, I won't have to at

all. You're such a brat." She leaned over to kiss me and ended

up on my lap with her nasty ass.

"You wanna fuck before you go in? Is that why you're

on my lap?" I kissed her neck.

131

"Maybe. You know I never rode a man while he was driving or even in a car. Can we do it?"

"Hell yea. Take these scrubs off and throw those ugly ass crocs away."

"I can't do it right now because you brought me to work fifteen minutes before I had to be here and we both know you ain't no minute man." She slid her tongue across my lips.

"Then why you bring it up. Look what you did and he ain't happy." My dick was hard as hell.

"Fine. Pull on a side street." She fell on the seat and made a call to someone at work to say she'll be a few minutes late. I shut the car off, slid my seat back and watched her remove her pants and underwear.

"Damn, I got a sexy ass girlfriend."

"And my man ain't too bad looking either. Especially with those different color eyes I love so much."

"It ain't my eyes you loveeee." I let a moan slip my lips when she maneuvered all the way down.

"I love all of you baby."

"Mmmmmm, damn ma. I be ready to cum every time you slide this good ass pussy on my dick."

"Sssssss. Yesssssss, you feel amazing." She moaned out. Her head went back and just like always she handled her business.

"Let me eat that real quick." I licked my lips as she sat in the other seat pulling her clothes up.

"Fazza, I'm already mad I gave you some. I'm going to be super tired now."

"So. Call out."

"Hell no. I got bills and..."

"I'll pay them for you. Matter of fact, move in with me." She stared and smiled.

"Maybe."

"What you mean maybe? You fuck around and come home to an empty house. Keep fucking with me."

"I love you Fazza and be safe out there." She ignored me and opened the door.

"I will. You want me to bring you lunch or dinner? I don't know what it's called when you work this late."

"Umm sure. I go to lunch at midnight. Bring me my favorite."

"I don't feel like smelling no damn tuna sub from Quick Check." That's the only place she ate them from and she knew they were open twenty-four hours because of the gas station connected.

"But you love me soooooo." She smirked.

"You gonna stop using how much I love you as an excuse to be a brat." She pulled me closer by my chin.

"I love you too." She kissed my lips.

"And don't forget my Doritos and soda." She closed the door and walked through the double doors. I can't believe outta all the women in my life, one has me strung the fuck out. I pulled off and went home to shower.

Kelly wanted to go out and since she's working I may as well join him. I set the alarm on my phone for 11:30. It'll give me time to get out the club, grab her sandwich and make it to her for break. It's the least I could do being Mazza and I are going outta town in a week.

****

"This is all my shit right?" I asked Shanta. I was at her house making sure I had everything so she wouldn't feel the need to call. With Ty in my life no other women needed access to me.

"Yea but why are you taking it?"

"Because I have a woman and the two of us don't need to be in contact."

"Whatever."

"I'm not about to explain shit to you. I'm out." I felt something hit my back and turned around to see tears coming out her eyes and the remote on the floor.

"Are you crazy?" I ran up on her and she backed into the wall.

"How could you find a woman knowing I'm still in love with you? Fazza, why would you do that?"

"Shanta, I told you already." And just like that she was in my arms with her tongue down my throat.

"Yo. What the fuck? I just told you." I pushed her off and walked to the door.

"Fuck her." She ran in front of me to block it and outta nowhere stuck her hands in my jeans. Yea, I should've backed away but the nigga inside didn't let me.

"Mmm hmm. You like the way this feels Fazza?" She kneeled down, took me in her mouth and next thing I know we fucking nonstop. I'm talking in the bed, on the floor and anywhere else we could get it in.

"Get me pregnant Fazza. Fuck yessssss." She screamed out and we both came. Right then I knew I messed up.

We used a condom all night and when I was leaving she got me hard again. We started fucking without one and I slipped up and came in her. I pushed her off, threw my clothes on, and hauled ass to the pharmacy. Thank goodness Walgreens was open.

I ran all around that store looking for a plan b. When I found it, I grabbed five. Hell yea she's taking all of them. I went to the register and ran into my worst nightmare. Tyler's mom. She instantly looked down at my hand and turned her face up.

"I'm glad she's not going to keep it."

136

"What?" I tossed them on the counter and waited for the lady to ring me up. No need to hide when her nosy ass clearly saw them.

"Ty told me about you not have protected sex. If you're buying this it means you slipped up. I pray it ain't too late when she takes it. I don't want a thug grand baby." I didn't say a word and rushed out the store and back to Shanta's. I opened all the boxes and placed the pills in my hand. If she saw them I guarantee we'd be fighting.

"Back so soon?" She opened the door naked and my dick grew. I wasn't even gonna go there with her.

"Come here Shanta." I picked up a glass out the dish drain, filled it with water and sat it on the counter.

"There's soda."

"I don't want it." I took my gun out and placed it on her temple.

"What are you doing?" Her hands went up.

"You knew exactly what you were doing when I came over. All that crying and faking about me having someone else was a trick for me to fuck you." She smirked.

"But I'm gonna get the last laugh." I cocked my gun back.

"You got one time to spit these pills out and I'm gonna splatter your brains all over this house."

"Fazza you know I wanted a baby with you." She started crying.

"And you know I said you weren't mother material. Take the fucking pills." She cried and whined for a good thirty seconds. When I hit her ass with the butt of the gun and split her eye, she took them real quick. I wasn't sure if they all went down but at least I knew one or two did. I don't care if they killed her. As long as she wasn't pregnant I could care less.

"Open your mouth." I used the tip of the gun to lift it wider and I saw no remnants of a pill.

"I HATE YOU!" She screamed as I picked my things up.

"You won't be the first or the last bitch to say those words. Peace." I slammed the door, went to my car and said a prayer.

God if you don't let Tyler find out, I promise to never cheat again. Amen.

I don't know if he heard me but I'm gonna be a praying ass nigga. If she finds out, I know for a fact she won't stick around. Or should I say, she'll try and leave because a nigga ain't letting her go.

Zia

"Zia what's wrong with you? Ever since you saw Jordan the night you moved somethings been up." My mom said and laid on my bed. I've been back and forth to work and straight home everyday. Even with the hurt tailbone, I couldn't let it stop me from making money. Whether my mom had my back or not, I needed my own place.

"I'm just stressed about not getting the house and giving up my apartment." She looked at me funny.

"I love staying here's but I'm used to being on my own."

"Did the realtor say why you didn't get the place?" I wanted so bad to tell her Jordan did it but she'd be ready to fight.

See the night Jordan left me at the apartment, he left me alone for a week and half like he said. When the time came to drive to Delaware for the opening of his new gym, I refused. I even stayed locked in my room that day because he'd probably snatch me up at work. I didn't need anyone at work calling the cops or being in my business.

140

Anyway, that Monday the realtor contacted me and said the sale fell through. I asked how and she told me, she had no idea. The papers were drawn up and the closing date was set. I knew then, Jordan somehow had a part in it. That's not all. He emptied out both of my bank accounts, sent me a screen shot of the zero balance and said the only way I'd get it back is to be with him. Guess who's a broke bitch? Yup. I'll start all over from scratch before I get with him again. I learned my lesson and have all my money put in an account under my mom's boyfriend Steph.

I wasn't worried about him taking anything because he had a lotta money. He too tried to get my mom out the projects and she still refused. No, they weren't out in the open yet, however I think the hood knew. Especially when he brought one of the dudes he knows over and he tried to kick it to my mom. I thought he was gonna kill the guy. I mean he had a gun at his head and everything.

She stayed with him that night and I was happy because the way he behaved, she had to calm him down and I'm not talking about smoking. We may be like best friends and have a great mother daughter relationship but there's no way in hell, I wanna hear them having sex.

"No she never said."

"What about your money at the bank? Zia that was a hella lot for them to lose."

"I know ma." I laid my head on her shoulder and cried. Nothing I did or said was gonna bring my money back or allow me to purchase the house unless I took Jordan back. Sometimes I think maybe I should go back to ho him but what happens if he takes it again because he's mad? My mom lifted my head and went to answer the door.

"You got company."

"Me?" I wiped my eyes because I don't have any friends and Jordan won't come here so who could it be.

"Clean yourself up first." I looked down at myself and laughed. I had on some ashy black sweat pants, with a green holy T-shirt, some orange socks and a scarf on my head.

"I'm ok."

"Alright. Don't say I didn't tell you." She smiled and went in her room. I heard the door shut and stepped in the living room to find Mazza standing there looking like a meal. I covered my chest because I didn't have on a bra.

"What are you doing here?" He grabbed my hand, led me out the door, and made me get in his truck, all without saying two words.

"I'm good bro. Yea she right here." He glanced over and smiled as he backed out. I was so uncomfortable in my attire.

"You look fine. Plus, I've see you naked and that beats any bad day you're having." My entire face must've turned two shades of red. I sat back and enjoyed the ride.

I ended up falling asleep and by the time I woke up we were passing a sign that read welcome to Virginia. I turned my neck quickly and noticed a few bags in the backseat. When did he stop or did he come with them? Whatever the case, I asked no questions and let my mouth hang open when he pulled up into some hotel that overtook the entire street.

"You look fine. Let's go." He opened the door, grabbed the bags and waited for me.

"Hi Mr. Chambers." Some guy said and took the bags.

"How are you?"

"I'm good. Is my room ready?"

"Yes sir. The top floor is all yours." He took my hand in his and led me to the elevator. The whole ride up, I looked down on the beautiful lobby and garden through the glass elevator.

"We're here." I stepped off and smiled. There were roses in front of the door. He handed them to me and kissed my cheek.

"This weekend is all about you." Once the door opened, I didn't wanna move pass the threshold. Everything was white and here I am dressed like a bum off the street. He noticed my nervousness, and bent down to remove my slippers and socks.

"It's so nice I don't wanna touch anything."

"Come on." He closed the door and took me in the bathroom. There was water filled to the top of the tub, rose petals, small tea lights and the moon was shining through the sky window.

"Mazza, why did you do all this for me?" I was amazed and shocked. He wasn't my man, had a girl and still made sure to make me smile.

"A little birdie called and informed me of all your troubles." He lifted my shirt over my head.

"I figured a nice getaway is exactly what you need." He had me step out my pants and helped me in the tub. I should've been embarrassed but I wasn't.

"The water feels really good and I definitely need this time to relax." I let my head rest on the back and closed my eyes. A minute or so later, soft music played through the speakers. It didn't take long for me to dose off.

****

"Z, time to get up." I opened my eyes and started shivering. The water was cold.

"I didn't mean to fall asleep."

"It's all good." He let some water out and refilled it with warm.

"If I forget to say it, thank you." He began washing me up and his touch was gentle and loving.

After he finished, he handed me a towel, helped me out, and he carried me in the room. There was food, a pair of pajamas and champagne. He let me down and I looked at him. Who is this man and if he has a woman, why is he here with me?

"I had no idea what you wanted to eat so I had them bring one of everything." I just broke down crying.

"I can send it all back." I chuckled a little and sat on the bed.

"It's not that."

"Then what's wrong?" He kneeled in front of me.

"The day you met me, I had it all together you know. I was in the process of buying my first house, I had 50k in my account for the down payment and another 5k to furnish my place. When I left Jordan, he said if I don't take him back he'd make sure everything was taken away and guess what? He did exactly what he said. My back account is at a zero balance and-"

"He's not a man Z." He stood me up and wiped my eyes.

"A man won't take things away from a woman because she refuses to be with him. I can see if she cheated then ok and even then, why take it if you have the funds to replace it? Look at me." Our eyes met and once again our tongues found one another and began to have their own playtime.

"Shit, I can't do this." He backed away.

"I'm sorry. You have someone and I'm going through a lot." He nodded but never took his eyes off me.

"Let me take a cold shower." He left me standing there hot and bothered. What the hell are we doing?

I wanted Zia in the worst way but I didn't wanna have her like this. We both had a lot going on and sex would complicate things. I mean she's not with her ex and Riley's on her way out. I won't feel like it's cheating because once I smelled the cologne of another man, it made me single. I just had to break it off. Being she's dramatic as fuck, I'm waiting until the concrete evidence surfaces.

When Zia's mom called it shocked me. How did she get my phone number? It didn't take long to find out Steph gave it to her. Evidently, she witnessed the chemistry between her daughter and I and felt I'd be the one who could make her smile. Imagine my surprise when I showed up and it's exactly what she did. I thought she'd tell me to leave. Now here we are in this hotel alone, probably horny and desperately in need of some type of affection.

"I want you Mazza." I turned around and Zia was standing in front of me naked.

"I have a..." I tried to say girl but once those lips wrapped around my dick, anything I had to say got lost.

"Mmmm, Mazza. Can I be nasty with you?" She stared up at me and flickered her tongue in and out the tip. All I could do is nod my head as she juggled both balls in her hand and took me back in her mouth.

"Oh fuck!" She was sucking me off way better than Riley. My eyes were rolling, toes were curling and my nut had already began creeping up.

"Sssss, I'm gonna cum with you." I looked down and her fingers were in her pussy.

"Hell no." I grabbed her hand and held it as she jerked me off and drained me of all my kids.

"That's my job Z." I shut the shower off, had her stand on the bench that was next to the vanity, lifted her leg and went to work.

"OH MY GAWDDDDDDD!" She screamed and I could feel her nails breaking the flesh on my shoulder.

"Give it to me." I stuck my finger inside her tight hole, moved it around a little and watched her entire body go weak. I had to catch her because she was about to fall.

"You down to be nasty?" She nodded real fast and tried to catch her breath.

"I want you to give me head, while I eat your pussy upside down." With no questions asked, she let me flip her over and both of us were moaning. I almost fell back when she made me cum again. I didn't even know a woman could get a man to do that back to back.

"I want you right here." I told her and opened the balcony doors. Because this is the only room on the top, floor no one could see us.

"Mazza." I placed her hands on the rail, pulled her body closer to me like I was stretching her out, rubbed the tip of my dick on her lips and eased my way in. She was super tight.

"You ok?" I saw how white her knuckles turned from gripping the rails. I'm no small nigga so I'm sure she was tryna adjust.

"Yes."

"You sure?" I pounded harder.

"YESSSSSSS! Fuck yessssss." She shouted and her essence shot out all over my stomach.

"This my pussy now Zia. Don't you fuck no one else."
I placed my hands on her shoulders and penetrated her insides
deeper.

"You hear me. No other man will sniff this pussy." She
turned her head and bit down on my hand.

"Tell me."

"Mazza no other man will have me. Oh Godddddd.
Here I cum again. Ahhhhhh." I was amazed at the amount of
times she could cum.

"Ride me." I sat on the chair outside and watched her
contorted facial expressions as she bonded with my man.

"Yea Z. Just like that." She moved back and forth, in
circles and then started popping up and down.

"Hell yea Z. Fuck me harder." I smacked her ass and it
sent her into a frenzy. She started doing all types of tricks. I'm
talking about putting her pussy on the tip squeezing and
dropping harder. She opened her ass cheeks to give me better
access and I had to stop her to keep from cumming. The best
was her taking my hand to rub her clit as she sucked on the
fingers of my other one.

"Fuck me til I cry Mazza." I ain't never heard no shit like that but I did it. I stood her up, lifted one leg on the rail and drilled as deep as I could go. She screamed, scratched, bit, punched and whatever else she could do.

"Where you want this cum at?" I yanked her hair, had her face me and stuck my tongue in her mouth as I continued fucking her from behind.

"Right here." She pushed me back, dropped to her knees and almost had me screaming. The way she sucked my kids out took every bit of energy I had. She stood, sat on my lap and laid her head on my shoulder.

"Goodnight." She said and a few seconds later I heard her lightly snoring. I carried her to the bed, hopped in behind her and did the exact same thing.

****

"Got dammit Zia. I'm not gonna ever leave with you doing me like this." She and I stayed in this hotel all weekend. We did go out on Saturday to sight see and do a little shopping. She was scared to buy anything so whatever she touched, I purchased. I can't even tell you how many times she yelled and

152

tried to get me to put the stuff back. I didn't and it's safe to say, she wouldn't need to shop for months if she didn't want to.

"Then give it to me." She was giving me head in the shower.

"Fuckkkkk!" I fell against the wall and felt her placing kisses up my body. Every time she touched me I wanted to lay her back down and make love to her.

"I'm gonna miss you Mazza but I also know this was a weekend fling." I pulled her body into mine.

"I want more with you Z. It's just.-"

"I know you have a woman." She rolled her eyes.

"Let me explain something to you Zia." I washed both of us up and turned the water off. I handed her a towel and took her in the room.

"If I were happy with Riley, none of this would've ever happened." I waved my hand at the room.

"When I'm with someone, I'm with her. Unfortunately, it's come to my attention that she's cheating."

"So what you cheat back to make it even?" She started snatching her clothes.

"I don't feel like I cheated because in my eyes we're over. The only reason I haven't broken it off is because she's dramatic as fuck. I want the evidence in my hand, therefore she won't try and make me feel bad for leaving."

"Who cares if she's dramatic? If that's not where you wanna be, leave." I grinned.

"You're impatient I see." I stood there watching her get dressed.

"Mazza, I'm not saying you have to be my man or anything like that but I did have a wonderful time and wanna do it again."

"And we will."

"When?" She pouted and I sucked on her lips poking out.

"Call when you want me and I'll come to you, or you can come to me."

"I can?"

"Yup. When I say it's over in my eyes, I mean it."

"She better not get any of this." She unwrapped my towel and started waking my man up with her hand.

"After the wild and freaky sex we had, I don't want no one else." I said and her smile grew wide.

"You like that huh?" I started putting my clothes on.

"Whatever." She said and bent over to put her sneakers on.

"Remember what I said about no one being close enough to sniff you."

"No one wants me Mazza." I swung her around.

"Don't put yourself down." I made her look in my eyes.

"I love everything about your body. The way it makes me cum hard. The way it shakes when I make it cum. And this mouth does wonders." I kissed her lips.

"The conversations we had are fun, and interesting."

"Really?"

"Yup." I made her look at me again.

"Zia, I want to see where this takes us but I wanna go slow. We're both getting outta something and need time to heal. We can have fun in the process but I want you to tell me if we're going too slow, too fast or you're not interested. All I ask is you don't sleep with another man, and I won't sleep with another woman. When people start exchanging those type of emotions, feelings get involved."

"You have feelings for me Mazza?" I smiled.

"I definitely feel something for you and have since the first kiss. I just wanna clear things up at home before taking it further with you. Can you handle that?" She nodded her head yes and I hope she meant it. Her pussy is the best I've had but I'll forget about her just as fast if she sleeps with someone else.

"You pregnant?" Bridget asked when I walked into work.

"HELL NO!" I put my purse on the desk.

"Why would you ask me that?"

"Because you're glowing and you had me cover you all weekend. That's unlike you." I let a smile grace my face and had her close the door. Two other employees were working and I didn't want anyone hearing.

"Well. Do you remember the two twins that came here a while back?"

"You mean the one with the weird eyes, that shitted and clogged the toilet?" She turned her face up. The two of us cursed him out to each other for days after he left. Ignorant motherfucker.

"Yea, I remember. Please tell me you didn't link up with him."

"Not! But his brother is a different story." Another smile graced my face as the nasty and freaky things we did clouded my mind.

157

"Do tell." She sat down anxiously waiting for the scoop. Bridget is probably the only person I told some of my business to because the only friend I had is my mother. I considered her more than an associate but not a bestie.

I explained how he surprised and picked me up. I also told her about the shopping spree I tried to avoid. I appreciated the gesture but after going through the nonsense with Jordan I didn't want anyone purchasing anything for me. Not even a damn cup of coffee. Women who've been through this will understand.

"Ok girly. Are you sure you're not pregnant!"

"Positive. As nasty as we were, we took extra precaution. Granted, the first time we slipped up but he pulled out." I didn't tell her how I sucked those babies out. Too much information if you ask me and I know damn well not to tell a woman about the man's sex. They may wanna try it and Mazza's bedroom skills will make a bitch crazy. I'm not tryna kill no one over a man who's not mine but I will.

"Too bad."

"Huh?"

"I would love to see Jordan's face when you tell him you're with someone else." I leaned back in the chair.

"It won't be for a while." I blew my breath.

"Why?"

I continued telling her how he had a chick who's allegedly cheating. I also told her how he wants me to be patient and anytime I need to see him, all I had to do is call or go to him. At least, I know he's serious about not being with her. I mean he can't be if he invited me to where he lives, right? It's a possibility we'd run into her. Whatever the case, I'm not gonna get my hopes up because he may take her back. I hope he doesn't but that's always an option so I need to prepare myself for it.

****

It's been three weeks since I've seen or heard from Mazza. As crazy as it sounds, neither of us exchanged phone numbers. We were so engrossed in each other's company that it never dawned on us to do it. Therefore; I couldn't get in touch with him. I could get his number from Steph but I don't wanna appear to be a stalker. He did tell me to give him time to handle his homefront. I just wish it didn't take as long.

"Where you been Zia?" I heard behind me as I grabbed a glazed donut and coffee for a customer. Not wanting to cause a scene, I handed the items to the cashier and walked around the counter. I thought about ignoring him and closing the office door but who am I fooling? He'll act the hell up so I may as well get it over with.

"Come on Jordan." I took a seat at the table.

"We need to speak outside."

"Right here is fine."

"Outside." He now spoke through gritted teeth. I prepared myself for his mental and verbal abuse. I'm sure it's gonna be loud and obnoxious.

He opened the door and stepped out behind me. You'd think he hold it for the older lady entering but no. He allowed it to close and tried to snatch my arm but I pulled away quickly. I was not about to let him stop my circulation. It must've pissed him off because he had my back against the wall.

"How's the new house?"

"I wouldn't know because someone ruined it for me."
He smiled.

"All you have to do come home." I busted out laughing.

"We both know that's not my home and even if I thought it was, the sight of you sexing two women is still in my head."

"Fuck then bitches. I'll buy a new bed and redecorate the room." He didn't even have the decency to apologize for being caught.

"Jordan, do you love me?" I asked with a serious face.

"What kind of question is that?"

"A question I want you to answer."

"Of course, I do." I folded my arms because he was not convincing me one bit.

"What do you love about me?" He stood there looking stupid. I thought about Mazza's remarks. We were nowhere near loving each other but he appreciated my body, conversation and everything else about me.

"Why is that even relevant? We been together long enough for you to know what it is."

"I knew it." I pushed his chest.

"Knew what? What's wrong with you?"

"What's wrong with me is you don't love me. You like the control you had and I say had because I'm over it. How could you waste my time? It's my fault for loving you and thinking things would change seeing I'm independent and not with you for money."

"Independent?" He laughed as if were the funniest thing ever.

"Yes independent. You may have paid those small ass bills for me but I would've lived with candles and no cell had I known you'd throw it in my face. I had my own place regardless of the size. My own car, hoopty or not and I never asked you for anything. You don't have to say it but we both know I don't need you." I tried to walk past and he grabbed my arm.

"You can play the Miss Independent role all you want but the fact remains you're a hood rat from the ghetto looking for a come up like the rest of these bitches out here. Say what you want but the small things I did buy you had no problem

162

sporting. Those few pair of red bottoms, and expensive clothes no longer have tags and you're not with me for money, right?"

"Nigga those things were to accompany you to events. I didn't need or request any of it." I stared at him.

"You know what Jordan, I don't wanna argue. I'm at work and it's unprofessional for me to stand out here like this discussing personal issues. We just need to go our separate ways. You wanna control me and I want a man to be proud of the woman by his side. Not someone who's ashamed and has her pretending to be someone she's not. Goodbye Jordan."

"Nah, we're not over." Just as he leaned down to kiss me I heard loud music pull in the parking lot. His lips pressed against mine and I started to push him away.

"What up Jordan? This you?" I knew the voice and turned around to stare in the face of Mazza and his brother.

"Yea this my woman."

"She's a good look on you. See you around." I noticed the brother chuckle and shake his head.

"How do you know them?" I asked and watched as he turned his face up.

"I was gonna do business with them but the plans fell through."

"Those don't look like men you'd do business with. What's that about?"

"Nothing. Well finish this conversation another time." He walked off and left me standing there. I went to the door and some chick began storming in the direction of the store.

Whoever she was, she had on a pair of red bottoms, tight ass jeans, a fitted shirt and her makeup was on point. She screamed a bad bitch. I opened the door and stepped in behind her.

"MAZZA!" She shouted. I know damn well he didn't bring his girlfriend down here. When he turned around to respond, I knew it's exactly who she was. *Fuck my life!*

"What the fuck are you doing here Riley?" I yanked her arm and pulled her to the side. I saw Zia standing there with her arms folded.

"I followed you. What you mean why am I here?" I ran my hand over my face. It didn't matter she followed me because I wasn't doing anything. The fact she did bothered me because truth is, I came to spend time with Zia.

Over the last three weeks I was thinking about her constantly. We didn't have each other's number and I'm not on social media. It was fine with me because it would've been a distraction to me handling business. I can see me being on the phone with her all the time or even had her in Delaware fucking the shit outta each other. I didn't want her to miss out on more work; especially when she recently got that promotion.

Needless to say, Riley covered her tracks well but I'm not stupid. She came home a few more times with the same cologne lingering in her clothes, hopped in the shower and pretended to want sex. Now I could've been a dick and done it but I wouldn't get shit out of it. We had a good sex life but if you're sleeping with someone else, ain't no way you can perform 100% twice in a day for two different people. Not only that, I promised Zia I wouldn't sleep with anyone else and she did the same. Looks like the joke was on me because I show up to surprise her and she's kissing dude. It's all good because two can play that game.

"Why the fuck are you following me?" I tried not to be loud.

"Because the last time you came here, I didn't see you for three days. You claim it was work but I'm not stupid. Who is she?" She had her lips pouted and arms folded over her chest. I admit this woman used to be my weakness and seeing her this upset, used to make me give in but not anymore.

"Go home Riley."

"I'm not going anywhere. Wherever you go, I go. Fuck that." I shook my head.

"You're really pushing me."

"What are you gonna do? Huh?" She pushed me back a little and I had to calm myself down. Not that I condone her putting hands on me but now she doing it in public. I have to draw the line.

"Ima say this one time so hear me good." I moved closer and her back hit the window. She could tell by my facial expression how upset I was.

"Ummm, excuse me." I heard Zia's voice and backed up a little. I didn't even get a chance to warn Riley on what I was gonna do.

"I'm sorry to bother you but I have a store full of customers. Can you take this outside?" I looked behind her and it was quite a bit of people.

"Sure." I said. In those few seconds I don't know why but things went from bad to worse.

"Why the fuck are you asking us to leave? We're paying customers like the rest of them." Riley started causing a scene.

"Ma'am you haven't brought anything and once your situation is handled please feel free to return."

"Situation?"

"Let's go Riley. She's being nice." I grabbed her arm and she snatched it away.

"No fuck that Mazza. We were having a private conversation and this low budget, fake ass, wanna be manager is over here bothering us." I could see Zia tryna calm down.

"Oh shit now. Let me hit record." Fazza said walking up with his phone pointed at us.

"Ma'am I need you to leave before I contact the police."

"Call the cops bitch." And that was it. I don't know what it is about that word but it tends to piss women off.

"Sir, I'm gonna ask you nicely to escort her outta here." It's crazy how we spent an entire weekend together and she's addressing me as sir.

"Fuck you bitch. He ain't taking me nowhere."

"Yo Zia. I know you're not about to let her talk shit to you in your store." Fazza egging her on didn't help the situation at all.

"Oh you know this bitch Fazza?" She looked Z up and down.

"Figured you'd fuck a ghetto rat." Outta nowhere, Zia reached over and knocked the shit outta Riley.

"Yea Z. Get that bitch." I'm sorry to say but Zia was whooping Riley's ass.

"Fazza help me break this shit up."

"Hell no. Riley deserved that ass whooping." He was about to say something else until I gave him a look. He's not scared of me but he knew I wasn't playing.

Once we pulled them apart, I dragged Riley out the store. Fazza was in there tryna calm Zia down and I'm not sure it's working. The only thing is, as she looked out the window with her face turned up I can't tell if she's mad at me or Riley. She probably assumed we're still together and that may be true but there's no sex involved.

"Go home."

"I'm not going home Mazza and I want her dead." I laughed at her stupidity.

"Dead because she beat your ass? You had no business flipping on that woman. What's wrong with you?" She fixed

169

her hair and took the napkins out my hand to wipe her bleeding nose. Her left eye was swelling and she had a few scratches.

"Mazza somethings going on between us and I wanna know what it is." She ignored me telling her to leave, and the fact she just asked me to kill Zia because she got her ass whooped is mind boggling.

"Not here Riley. I'll be home in a few days."

"We'll enjoy Maryland together because I'm not going home."

"Fine. This the hotel I'm staying at. Give them my name and I'll be there soon." I started making my way towards the store.

"Where are you going?"

"I have to make sure the manager isn't going to press charges."

"I don't care if she does. Let's go Mazza. I want you to make love to me. I miss the way you touch me." I almost laughed in her face.

"I'll see you later.

"Mazza!" She yelled and ran over to me.

"I miss us, so hurry up." Her arms flew around my neck and she threw her tongue in my mouth before I could stop her.

"I'll be there soon Riley." I watched her go to the car and pull off before going in the store. The only people remaining were me, Faz, two employees and Zia who had her arms folded and hurt written on her face.

"Let me talk to you."

"No need." She went in the back and I followed, closing the door behind me.

"You ok?" She scoffed up a laugh.

"Nice of you to check on me after your girl. You know I thought you were different." I could see aggravation all over her face.

"What?"

"I believed you would handle your business at home, which is why I'm not even mad we haven't spoken but you're still with her."

"Says the woman who was kissing her ex when we pulled up."

"The difference is, I had just finished cursing him out and pushed him off. I told him to leave me alone because I thought the two of us were gonna hook up from time to time and I don't have sex with two men. But why did I do it when it's obvious you're still together."

"Let me explain Zia."

"Explain what? Explain how I'm most likely fired because of her? Or explain why she kissed you outside and you didn't stop her? Or wait, how she's not leaving and you told her to wait at the hotel for you?" She shook her head in disgust.

"Yea, I heard you because I walked out to tell you the cops weren't called and to make her leave."

"I wanted her to go Zia."

"So you have her meet at your hotel? Then she called me all types of names and bitches and you didn't even defend me. I know I'm not your woman but damn. I saw her talking shit and pushing on you and I came over. I didn't address it but it made her stop." I stared and saw how upset she was.

"Zia, I came to surprise you. I'm sorry she did all this and if you get fired I'll pay your bills." She sucked her teeth.

"I'll be broke and homeless before I allow any man to pay my bills."

"I didn't mean it like that. It's my fault she came so let me make it up to you." She plopped in the chair and used both her hands to rub her temples.

"Just go Mazza."

"Zia."

"I appreciate you coming to surprise me and offering to compensate me but one... she's here and you're still a couple so us spending time together isn't happening. And two... I'll have to suck it up and go back to Jordan." I snatched her out that seat fast as hell.

"Whether you're my woman or not, you got one fucking time for me to hear you with that nigga. Do I make myself clear?"

"Mazza you have a.-" I had the front of my thumb and the knuckle of my index finger on her chin.

"I don't give a fuck what I have. You heard what I said now play with me if you want." I kissed her lips and backed up.

"I'm gonna handle Riley, don't you worry about that. Have my pussy ready for tonight." I left her standing there with her arms folded and shock on her face. Maybe she didn't know how I got down but she'll learn soon enough. When I claimed something, it was mine to keep.

"What is going on with you Riley?" Evelyn said when I called her up on the way to the hotel.

"What you mean, what's going on with me?" I tossed the napkin on the other seat. The bitch made my nose bleed but I got something for her.

"First, you started putting hands on Mazza, and now you're cheating on him. Today you pick up and follow him into another state knowing the type of work he does. You cause a scene at a Dunkin Donuts with a woman who only asked y'all to argue outside and end up in a fight. Are you tryna make him leave you or even find out what you're doing?" I sucked my teeth because I felt like she was judging me.

"Get mad all you want but you're causing unnecessary drama for no reason. If you want to stay with Mazza, I suggest you get it together and work on your relationship."

"I'm trying to Evelyn but he's not interested. We haven't had sex in weeks and..."

"Why does it matter? You're having sex with someone else."

"I still want him Evelyn." I parked at the hotel and went inside.

"Ok what are you going to do about it? Have you thought of a way to win him back?" I didn't say anything because me following him should be enough for him to know I want us to work.

"I haven't done anything to win him back and I don't know what I'm going to do about it." I blew my breath and continued observing my eye in the bathroom mirror.

"Then his cousin is after me."

"His cousin?" She sounded shocked, as she should because no one was aware that the two of us even knew each other.

"Yes. The bitch Shakim had two kids by, is his cousin." I rolled my eyes thinking about the last conversation me and the bitch had.

"WHATTTTT!" She shouted.

"Yes and I asked why didn't she tell him that she knew who I was, and her response was because he loves you. Also, how would he feel knowing you dated his mentor? Oh and he's going to kill you if he finds out you had anything to do with his death. She went on and on.-" She cut me off.

"Back up Riley. What does she mean if you had anything to do with Shakim's death? Why would she think that? Please don't tell me you did?" I remained quiet.

"RILEY?"

"I was about to answer you damn. Hold on." I walked over to the door and saw Mazza and his ignorant ass brother walking in.

"Let me call you back. Mazza just got here."

"Call me back too Riley. I wanna know what she's talking about." She shouted.

"Alright Evelyn." I hung up and a text message came through from my guy friend. It was a picture of me sucking his dick. I smiled because he was blessed too and I enjoyed giving him head. Not sure I should've allowed him to take a photo but who cares? He doesn't know Mazza.

I deleted the message and sat on the couch as Mazza moved around the suite. Fazza sat across from me and stared. I swear I hated him. He stayed in our business and always accused me of being sheisty. Mind you, I never did anything to him. He's just as crazy as the rest of these people out here.

I heard the bathroom door close and went to scrolling in my phone. He and I never have anything nice to say to each other. I'm not gonna even pretend to wanna hold a conversation.

"Can I ask you a question?" I rolled my eyes and ignored him.

"I'm gonna ask anyway just because." He made a loud burp and scooted to the edge of his seat.

"Do you love my brother? I mean, like really love him?" I looked up.

"Even though the answer should be obvious, I'll entertain it." I sat my phone on the couch.

"I am in love with your brother. I want his kids and to marry him but he claims not to be ready." He snickered.

"Did you ever take the time out to think maybe he doesn't want those things with you?" He cracked a smile.

"It's been over five years and here you are ringless, and babyless."

"I'm glad you brought this up because it's exactly why I followed him. I know he's cheating on me and when I find out who she is, I'm gonna kill her." He stared directly at me as he sipped on his water. After he finished, he sat the bottle on the table, leaned on his knees with his elbows and clasped his hands together.

"We both know my brother isn't a cheater and let's say he did step out." He smirked. Is that a clue or him insinuated he already did? If anyone knows what Mazza is doing, he damn sure did.

"Why would you be upset when it's clear you're out doing your own thing."

"Excuse me." I stood up and placed my hands on my hips.

"Bitch, you know better than to stand over me. You better sit yo ass down and take it down a notch." I did what he said because Mazza may be crazy but he's the calm one. Fazza just don't give a fuck and I don't ever wanna be on his shit list.

"Like I was saying. You've been moving funny and if I notice it, my brother has. Let me leave you with a little advice." Now he stood over me.

"I want my brother to kick you to the curb because I can't stand you. But that's neither here or there." He laughed.

"My advice to you is whatever or whoever you're doing, better not ever come to light because both of you will be buried six feet under."

"Did you threaten me?"

"I'm just saying." He shrugged and went in the bedroom with Mazza, who went straight in there after using the bathroom.

I sat on the couch thinking about what Fazza said. Did they know what I was doing and who it's with? Could I leave the man alone, or should I? There were so many thoughts running through my head, I grabbed my things and left. Yup, I drove all the way home to try and come up with ways to make things right between us again. I'm still gonna find out who he's sleeping with and when I do she better be prepared for a fight.

"Let's go." I snatched Zia up out the bed at her mom's place. After Riley left, I could care less where she was and made plans to let her sit in the hotel room alone all weekend.

"I'm not going anywhere with you. Go back to your girlfriend." I placed her on my shoulders and let her punch me in the back a few times.

"Don't send her home pregnant." Her mom yelled out.

"Oh my God ma. Are you serious?"

"Yup. You're upset, which means y'all about to have makeup sex. No one straps up for that." I busted out laughing.

"I'll let you know if I leave my seed in her." I chucked up the deuces and walked out. A few people were staring because Zia was cursing and tryna break loose. All she did was turn me on more.

"If you get out this truck I'ma fuck you up." I gave her a look letting her know I wasn't playing. She folded her arms and pouted.

"You hungry?"

"No. Take me home."

"I missed you Z."

"Whatever." She leaned her head on the window.

"Don't whatever me. Look at me." I turned her face and noticed how watery her eyes were. Was she really feeling me like that? I mean, I've been growing stronger feelings for her too but damn.

"Z, I didn't break up with her yet and I'm sorry for what she did in your store. The kiss was unexpected but I promise you, I didn't sleep with her."

"Did you lay in the same bed?" I blew my breath in the air.

"Yes."

"So you slept with her."

"Technically, yes. Sexually, no. I couldn't do it." My eyes were going back and forth, from her to the road.

"Why not? I mean y'all still a couple."

"Because she's definitely fucking someone else and the only woman on my mind was you." She turned back to face me.

"I wanted you there when I woke up and went to bed. I wanted to speak to you on the phone or even FaceTime you but we never exchanged numbers. Actually, it was better that way because you would've been a distraction."

"Why is that?" She smiled.

"Because I know for a fact, I wouldn't have gotten anything done. Zia, I don't know when my feelings became strong for you or why but you are definitely the only woman I want."

"Pull over."

"For?" I questioned and did it anyway.

"For this." She pulled her pajama shorts and panties down, maneuvered her way in my lap, unbuttoned my jeans, found what she wanted and slid down.

"I for sure missed this." I said. We started kissing as she grinded in circles on me.

"Me too baby." She sucked on my neck and let her hands roam under my shirt.

"Shit Z. You gotta get up. I ain't had none so I'm ready to cum."

"Wait! I'm cumming too. Hold on." She dug her nails in my chest and unfortunately, both of us released at the same time.

"I couldn't hold it." I placed a few kisses on her neck.

"We can go to the pharmacy." We kissed a few more times before she lifted herself off.

I handed her napkins out the glove compartment and waited for her to clean up. Shockingly, she did the same for me. Riley, has never done that. She'll get in the shower with me and all that but she won't bring a rag to clean me off if we have spontaneous sex. Another plus for Zia in my book. I looked at her, smiled and headed to a different hotel. Hell yea, I'm fucking her all weekend.

****

"When you coming back?" Zia asked and laid in the bed with a sheet in between her legs. Instead of staying the weekend, I stayed the entire week. When she went to work, I was out doing other things and checking up on employees. I trusted everyone and my money was always right but since she was working there wasn't anything else to do.

"I'm tying up some loose ends and I'll be back this weekend." I climbed in the bed with her.

"Get dressed. I have a surprise for you."

"No more surprises Mazza. My feet hurt and my pussy is super sore." I fell back laughing. She and I had sex everyday and her feet hurt because yesterday when she was off, we went shopping.

"I thought you loved the dick surprises."

"Oh I do but I need a break sometimes. If you lived here, I'd only give you some once a week."

"Bullshit." She started laughing and stood up."

"You're right. That has me strung out and ready to return to Delaware with you." I walked over to her.

"If you wanna come, I'll get you a place." She stared at me. I was serious about being with her but Riley wasn't giving up and I needed to let her know in person we're done. I probably should take some time to be alone since Riley and I were together for so many years but being with Zia felt right. I didn't wanna wait and she find someone else.

185

"You have loose ends and once they're tied up we can revisit this conversation."

"Remember you said that." I carried her in the bathroom, showered with her and checked out. I placed our things in the car and pulled off.

"Where are we going?"

"Do you know what a surprise is?" I smiled and continued driving.

"Yes but."

"No buts baby. Trust me. You're gonna love it."

"I better." She pouted as usual but sat there enjoying the music and ride.

I stopped in front of a house, parked and ran over to her side. She seemed confused but didn't ask any questions. I took her hand in mine, closed the door, grabbed the keys out my pocket and went to the front. I could see her admiring the lawn and the few houses in the cult de sac. I slid the key in the lock, let the door open and stopped her before going in.

"Zia." I made her look at me because she was smelling the roses sticking out the grass.

"Yea babe."

"I know you've gone through a lot in this short time we've known one another, but I've grown strong feelings for you. I want you to know that I'm doing everything to be with you, even if you can't see it." She smiled.

"I know it's complicated right now and I appreciate you still being around."

"About that. Mazza, I'm not a side chick and I deserve more than..." I kissed her to cut her off.

"Exactly! Which is why I sent a text to Riley a few days ago telling her it was over and to get all her things out the house." She looked shocked.

"I'm sorry for putting you in a position like that and it'll never happen again."

"Mazza, you live in Delaware and I live in Maryland. It's not far but I don't want a long-distance relationship. I want you here all the time."

"And you're gonna have me." I led her in the house and watched as the tears flowed down her face.

There was a Congratulations on your new home banner I had made up, hanging. Her mom, Steph, Fazza and Tyler were standing there and so was the Bridget chick who worked at Dunkin Donuts. I had her mom get the living room and one of the bedrooms furnished so she had something to start off with. The rest she could order whenever.

"Mazza, I can't accept this." She wiped her eyes.

"You can and you will. I mean your mom's cool and all but my woman needs her own place. And before you start, here's the paperwork with everything in your name; including the new Infinity car in the garage."

"You didn't." She rushed out and banged on the garage door to open. I pressed the button and watched her face light up as the black on black car showed. She ran over to me and jumped in my arms.

"I'm gonna fuck you so good when you come back, you're gonna put a ring on it."

"He needs to put one on it now. It's clear you done some freaky shit to him if he buying you all this." I thought my brother had a smart ass mouth but him and her mom were in a race for that. I pulled her close and whispered in her ear.

"Hell yea you're gonna fuck me good. I'm digging in that ass again too." I winked and she smirked. We tried anal and fell in love with it.

"At this point, I'll let you put it in my ear if you wanted."

"That's my nasty girl. Let's go see the rest of the place."

"Bro, I'm hungry. Tyler ate up all the food."

"Fazza, you keep blaming me and I promise you won't get none for two weeks." I loved Tyler for him because she played no games and gave it back to him each time.

"Hi, I'm Tyler, Fazza's soon to be ex." She rolled her eyes and he waved her off.

"This dick too big and too good for you to pass it off to someone else so stop lying to yourself."

"And this right here." She pointed in between her legs.

"Will lay up under someone else if you don't stop.-"
She never finished her sentence because Fazza wrapped his
hand around her throat and the other one yanked her head back.

"Stop fucking saying that Ty. I swear you're gonna
make me kill you." He smashed his mouth on hers.

"Do that again and I'm tasing your ass." She jumped on
his back and bit down on his neck."

"Can someone call animal control for this stray
monkey?" All of us just shook our heads.

"Are they always like this?" Z asked.

"Every second of the day. Come look around." Fazza
and Ty were still playing and her mom was sitting on Steph's
lap. It seemed like all of us had a good woman for the
moment.

"I can't wait to fill this house up with furniture. My
checks aren't big but a little at a time is fine." I stood behind
her as she stared down in the huge backyard from the balcony
in the master bedroom.

"There's a credit card with your name on it, in the
nightstand." She turned to look at me.

190

"There is no limit. Buy what you want."

"Mazza, the house and car are enough."

"Nothing is too much for you. All I ask is for you to be faithful and the world is yours."

"Mazza, I promise to be faithful and cater to all your needs. But understand, I won't be a fool and will leave all of this behind if you cheat or hurt me."

"How can I hurt the woman I'm falling for?" She blushed, walked over to the door and locked it.

"How about a quickie before you leave?"

"Shit, you don't have to ask me twice." I started unbuckling my jeans but she stopped me.

"Let your woman take care of you." Not even a minute later she was on her knees making me bite my lip to stop from moaning. *Life couldn't get no better than this.*

"So you fucked around and fell in love, huh?" I asked my brother when we dropped Ty off. We just returned from Maryland and had to do some running around.

"Not yet but my feelings are definitely involved."

"I'd say. You buying her houses and shit."

"That's because the fuck nigga Jordan stole all the money out her bank account and did some shit to make the sale of the house she was about to buy, fall through."

"Nah. He ain't do no fuck shit like that." I shook my head in disbelief.

"I thought the same thing until I happened to hook up with the same realtor Zia had."

"She came out and told you?"

"Yes and no." I looked at him.

"When Zia's mom told me what happened, I felt bad and started looking for places to help her out. The lady took me to the house and explained how a woman was supposed to close on it and a few days before, some guy called and said she was a felon and had committed a murder. They never bothered looking into it and believed him."

"That's fucked up."

"What's more fucked up is he told her if she took him back he'd fix it all." I shook my head.

"Why he want her back if he sleeping with all those women?"

"I asked her the same thing. She said he liked having control over her."

"He beating on her?" I turned at looked at him.

"Nothing like that but she did say he yoked her up. And the day we rolled up on them, he was threatening her."

"What the fuck wrong with him?"

"I don't know but she my girl now and ain't no way he's about to make any more threats to her." He had a grin on his face.

"What about this one?" I asked when he pulled into his driveway. I left my car here when we drove to Maryland. Riley had her truck parked front and center

"I broke up with her already."

193

"And she still here?"

"I told her to bounce. She didn't listen so of course she's gonna make me show my ass." We both got out.

"Well let me use the bathroom first." He opened the door and both of our mouths fell open.

"SURPRISE!" She shouted. There was a pregnancy test in her hand and my mom was standing there shaking her head.

"Ugh, I'll wait to use the bathroom." He turned to look at me but I bounced. You won't have me caught up in that shit.

****

"You sure you're not pregnant yet?" I asked Ty as she barely bounced up and down. Usually she's riding my shit like a jockey and lately she claims it hurts.

"Not that I know of. Hold on Fazza. I'm cumming again." Instead of stopping she turned around cowgirl style, stood on her feet and rode me real good. She stopped a few times but made sure I got mine.

"You have to stop swallowing my kids, if you're gonna have my kids."

194

"I can't stand you." She smiled and kissed me.

"I want you to find out." I flipped her over and kissed down her stomach.

"Ok baby. Oh shittttttt." I clamped down on that clit and went to work. I loved hearing her moan, feeling her scratch, punch and bite me. And scream how much she loved me.

See Tyler isn't a woman who ain't about shit. She had a good head on her shoulders, had her own everything and didn't take my shit. Most women are terrified of me and I loved that too. However, a woman who stands up to a man only proves she won't allow anyone to treat her like shit.

"I love you so much Fazza. Yes baby." Her cream oozed in my mouth and I swallowed every drop. I mean why not? She's my baby mama, we basically live together and she's going to be my wife. It's only right for me to do it, when she swallows my seeds too.

"I think I may be pregnant." She said tryna catch her breath.

"Why you say that?"

"It's never hurt as much having sex and sometimes it's painful. Even I know when that happens it means somethings up."

"We need to know for sure before I tell my mom."

"You think she'll be happy?" She rolled over and rested her head on my chest.

"Hell yea." She glanced up at me.

"Why you say it like that?"

"Man please. No one thought I'd ever have kids."

"Oh." She laughed but I was dead serious.

"Yea they say I have issues and my mouth is reckless."

"Ya think?" She pulled the covers up.

"Don't come for me Ty. You have your own shit too."

"It only shows when you cut up."

"Anyway, ma dukes will be excited, especially since Mazza's expecting."

"Oh my God Really? Zia is such a good match for him and she's nice. I love the way they are with each other." I sat up. I expected her to get excited because the two of them hit it off right away, or should I say after her and my brother came out the room. All of us knew what they were doing which is why we had our own party downstairs with Steph and her mom.

Anyway, they started discussing the line of work they do and some other shit I thought was corny. They exchanged phone numbers and even texted each other on the drive back. I ain't have an issue with that because she's my woman and eventually, they'd be around one another soon enough.

"I hate to bust your bubble but Zia is not the one having his baby."

"I'm confused." She turned over and let her head rest on her arm.

"Don't go running your mouth either."

"I won't but I'm still confused."

"Zia's not having his baby. Riley is." She covered her mouth and sat up.

"Wait! I thought he broke up with her. What am I missing?"

"He did. However, when we got to the house she was there with my mom and a pregnancy stick in her hand."

"What did your mom say?"

"I don't know because I didn't even wait to hear the ending." She sat there shaking her head.

"The look on her face was disappointing because Mazza told my mom before we went to Maryland he didn't want her anymore."

"Wait! How is he expecting with her and tryna be with Zia?"

"Didn't your special ass just hear me say, she yelled surprise when he walked in? He ain't know." She popped me in my mouth.

"I done told yo ass to stop hitting me."

"What you gonna do about it?" She was on her knees with her arms folded.

"Keep this dick out yo life."

"That's fine. At least, I don't have to do jaw exercises anymore."

"My dick is big right?"

"I'm going to bed Fazza." She slammed her body on the bed and rolled over.

"That's what I thought. Scoot yo ass over here." I pulled her closer and rested my arm on her stomach.

"I'm happy you're having my baby."

"We don't even know if I am."

"You can't take this dick like before. Trust me, you are." She elbowed me in the stomach.

"Keep playing Ty." She turned over.

"I know we play around a lot with the fake fighting and shit but are you sure this is what you want?" She slid her index finger over my lips. I saw nothing but love in her eyes for me.

"If it's with you, absolutely." Just by the way she looked at me, I know she is the only woman who had my heart.

"I love the hell outta you Fazza and I love you even more for not falling victim to temptation with these ho's."

"They don't have nothing on you babe."

"As long as I have you, they sure don't." She kissed my lips and snuggled under me. I said another prayer to God that we never run into Shanta together. That bitch has been off the hook texting and threatening me about telling whoever my girl is. I swear if I lose Ty, I'm gonna kill her.

"Have you seen Mazza?" Zia asked when I answered the phone. It's been two weeks since we met and the two of us spoke almost everyday. She was cool as hell and I enjoyed talking to her. Dealing with two crazy brothers can take a toll on you. Especially, when you're with the maniacal one like me.

"I saw him yesterday when the two of them stopped by. Is everything ok?" I could hear the frustration in her voice.

"Yea, I just miss him."

"When's the last time you spoke to him?"

"The day he left." I stayed quiet because I'm sure the reason he didn't talk to her is Riley. Fazza told me ever since she told Mazza about the pregnancy he's been stressed out and she's been floating on air.

"I know he told me to be patient and that he's tying up loose ends but damn. Should I be worried?" She asked and I was still being careful with my words.

"I'm sure he's doing exactly what he told you. Don't work yourself up Zia. The last time it was three weeks and I know for a fact he was out handling business because Fazza went with him."

"If you say so?" I felt bad because I'm lying to her. I wanted to tell her but Fazza made me promise to let his brother do it. I wish he hurry up because this lying shit ain't for me.

"Soooooo, are you pregnant?"

"I'm scared to find out Zia."

"What? Why? You said he's excited."

"He is but somethings off."

"I'm lost." I started to tell her why I felt that way.

"Ok so a while ago, maybe two months I can't even remember because with him, time is flying by. I never know what day it is."

"True." She laughed.

"Ugh ahh, heffa. Don't come for my man."

"Whatever with his disgusting ass." The day she told me he messed the toilet up in the store, I almost peed on myself. Then he had the nerve to get upset because the worker told. I didn't expect no different from his ignorant ass.

"Anyway." I rolled my eyes even though she couldn't see me.

"A while back, I was working my 12-hour shift and he dropped me off. He came back with my lunch being his normal self. The next day, he picks me up from work, takes me home and I go straight to sleep. I have no idea where he went but he came back over pissed off. I asked what was wrong and he said nothing."

"Maybe it wasn't."

"That's what I said and left it alone. A couple of days went by and he started coming out of his funk but then his phone starts going off all hours of the night, text messages are coming through and so forth. It's odd to me because once we made it official all of it stopped."

"Maybe it was emergencies."

"I thought the same until I checked the messages."

"What did they say? Who were they from?"

"Funny thing is, they were private calls and the text messages were only mad face emojis, laughing ones and sometimes crying ones. Never an actual text."

"What you think they mean?"

"I have no idea but last night, I told him I'm happy temptation didn't get the best of him and his entire demeanor changed."

"What you mean?"

"I don't know. It's like he went from excited to nervous. Like he's hiding something."

"That is odd but don't go jumping off the deep end. Has any bitches approached or called you?" She asked.

"No."

"That's good because we all know a scorned hateful bitch will tell."

"True!"

"Just talk to him Tyler. It may be nothing." I agreed and stayed on the phone with her a little longer. I couldn't help but feel sad when she hung up. I really hope Mazza tells her before she finds out on her own.

****

"Baby, can I use your car today?" I screamed out to Fazza in the shower. I was going to the doctor to find out about

203

my pregnancy. I wanted him to come but he was so excited about having a kid, I didn't want to him disappointed if it hadn't happened yet.

"Yea, I'll take yours. That piece of shit needs to be upgraded."

"There's nothing wrong with my car Fazza." I leaned on the wall in the bathroom. I had a 2016 Honda Accord fully equipped and I loved it. He wanted me to get a newer one. Talking about his woman needs to be in all new shit.

"Whatever. Gimme a kiss." I walked over and slid my tongue in his mouth.

"Let me get some real quick." He tried to drag me in the shower.

"I got you later baby. My mom is waiting." I was struggling trying to get away.

"Yo, don't let her fake bible having ass, talk bad about me." I busted out laughing.

"Never baby. I got your back."

"And my front." He pushed my hand towards his growing erection.

"Tonight baby."

"It's on later."

I kissed him again and grabbed everything I needed for the doctors. My mom was calling me nonstop to pick her up because she wanted to eat first. I love her to death but she could be judgmental and a handful at times. I know it's from missing my dad but I need a break.

I parked in front of her house and blew the horn. She came strolling out and I couldn't help but smile. For her to be almost fifty, she looked good for her age. She ate healthy, worked out as much as possible and still held a nine to five. I hope at that age I'm as energetic as her.

We went to the diner first, and then drove to the doctors talking about life, and a few times she tried to come for Fazza but I cut it short. She may not care for him and the same goes for him but I do expect them to respect each other. I had butterflies in my stomach, anticipating if I'm expecting or not.

"Are you happy?" She asked about the doctor confirming my pregnancy. We left not too long ago and the entire ride, we both remained silent. It's as if we were both in our own thoughts.

"Actually I am." She rolled her eyes.

"How many times have you tried since you took the plan b?" I pulled in front of her house.

"Plan B?" I questioned. I was confused as hell.

"Yea, I saw him in the store buying a few of those pills and I told him, I was glad you didn't keep it. I will love my grand baby but I do not want him or her growing up like him." I was flabbergasted, shocked and most of all hurt to hear the words leaving her mouth.

I know for a fact I've never taken a pill to terminate a pregnancy so who did he buy them for? He told me and I quote, *"If you take a plan b, miscarry by accident or get an abortion I'll kill you."* I mean, why would he tell me that if he's impregnating other women?

"Oh that. I wasn't ready." I'm not going to admit anything until I find out the truth. She hated him and I wouldn't put it past her to make the story up. Plus, I know it would probably give her satisfaction to know I'd leave him if he was cheating.

"As long as you're ready, I'm behind you 100%." She kissed my cheek.

"I'm happy for you Tyler and your dad would be too." She closed the door and I watched her go in.

I drove straight to Fazza's house but he wasn't there. As I sat in the car, I sent him a text asking where he was and he told me, he'd be home shortly. I was sort of happy because it gave me time to figure out how to ask the question. I can't be certain my mother is lying, but there was no proof either. The least I could do is give him the benefit of the doubt.

I thought about asking Zia what she thought since she and I became close but right now I'm embarrassed more than anything. I don't want to tell anyone if it's not true. Not that she'd judge but still.

I reached for my purse in the back because my mom sat in the front and told me she wasn't holding it. I ended up having to open the back door and get it because it fell over, knocking my stuff out. I hated when that happened because you'd have to dig under the seats to get your things like I am

now. The only difference is, I found what I wasn't looking

for. *I'm gonna kill him.*

"Shanta, you gotta stop texting and calling me in the middle of the night. Matter of fact stop calling me period." I told her outside the mall. Unfortunately, I ran into her picking up a pair of sneakers for Ty. I hated those damn crocs she wore to work so I picked her up a few of the new air max's. They say these are good on your feet.

"Is the misses getting upset?"

"Nah because she doesn't have shit to worry about."

"Then why does it matter?" She tried to look in one of the bags.

"Because I said so bitch. Keep fucking with me and Ima stop by your mama house and tell her where to find your body."

"You'll kill me Fazza?" She had a frightening look on her face.

"If you ruin my relationship with the misses, I'm gonna decapitate your body and send your mother a piece, everyday until she gets it all." She covered her mouth and backed up.

See Shanta's been around long enough to know how I get down. Never mind, I've done the decapitating and sending body parts to someone before. My brother and I try to be creative when we do kill. Too many people shoot and that's it. Sometimes a quick death requires a shooting but when there's no rush, you can take your time and do whatever. That's the beauty in being a killer.

"What's up babe?" I answered and opened my car door.

"Come to your house. I have something to show you."

"I'm on my way." I smiled because she's probably gonna show me an ultrasound photo. She must be outta her mind if she thought for one second, I didn't know her whereabouts. I didn't go in the doctor's office because her nosy ass mom was there. I was hoping she didn't mention the plan b shit to Ty and she must not have, because my girl didn't bring it up. Ty is definitely not the type to hold anything in. I hung up and answered when it rang again.

"Yo where you at?" Kelly asked as I put the bags in the trunk.

"Out. Why?" His tone stopped me from giving my whereabouts.

"Swing by." Something was definitely up. He never says swing by.

"Where you at?"

"The trap on 16th. See you soon. Oh, and bring Mazza."

"Be there shortly." I jumped in the car and called my brother.

"What's good?" He answered right away.

"Mazza we were talking." I heard Riley bitching as usual in the background.

"We got a problem on 16th."

"On my way." He disconnected the call. I used my Bluetooth to call Ty. She wanted me to come home but right now we had to get Kelly.

"Hello." She answered with an attitude.

"I'll be home shortly."

"Fazza we need to talk." Now her tone was fucked up. What the hell is going on today?

"Something happened to Kelly."

"Ok soon as you're done get here."

"Yo, What the fuck is good?" I barked. This morning we were good and now, she had major attitude.

"Fine. Since you have better things to do." I heard the doorbell in the background.

"Fazza, I told you not to cheat on me. Didn't I?" I pray she didn't know about Shanta.

"Ty, I'm not into playing games. Say what's on your mind."

"Hold on. Who's ringing your doorbell like that?" I pulled over and tapped on the app that shows my house. When I saw who stood out there, my mouth hit the floor. How did this motherfucker know where I lived?

"DON'T OPEN THE DOOR TY!" I shouted but, on the screen, you could see the phone in her hand on the side of her.

"TYYYYYYY." I yelled and just as she put the phone back to her ear, she put her hand on the doorknob.

"Can I help you?" I busted a U-turn.

"Nah, but your man can. Let's go bitch."

"There you go running off again." Riley whined when I hung up with Faz.

"We weren't talking about shit Riley."

"Mazza what's going on with you? We're having a baby and you're not even excited." I turned and moved closer to her.

"That's because I'm not sure if it's my baby." Her entire facial expression changed.

"Excuse me." She put her hands on her hips.

"Oh you thought I didn't know about the other guy?"

"Mazza."

"Mazza what? I smelled him on you a few times Riley so don't deny it. But what I don't get is why you did it? I gave you everything, never bothered you about working and sexually, we had sex all the time. What was slacking?" Were my feelings hurt? Absolutely. We've been together way too long for it not to. She may have been a nag and a stalker but I dealt with it so long, I was used to it. Yea, I made plans to leave her but not over cheating.

214

"Mazza, I..." She was tryna come up with the words.

"Do you know why I never came in you and when I did, made sure you popped those pills?" She didn't say anything.

"It's because after a few years you started changing and I didn't wanna bring a kid into that."

"You know I wanted to be married. Mazza you think I don't know about you and the other chick?" Its funny how she's tryna throw shit at me to cover up her infidelity.

"What other chick Riley? Huh? You accused me of sleeping with someone else and the entire time you been with another nigga."

"Come on baby. This is supposed to be a great time for us." She attempted to wrap her arms around my neck but I moved out the way.

"Riley, I told you it was over and I meant it. Just because you announced this pregnancy, nothing's changed." I walked to the door to leave.

"So you're gonna make me a single mother?" I chuckled.

"After you deliver, we'll get a test and go from there. As far as you being a single mom, you'll be single but my kid, if it's mine will have both parents in his or her life."

"Mazza how would your mom feel about you leaving me pregnant and alone?" She placed her hands on her hips. They used to be close and Riley knew, how my mom felt about us having a kid or kids. She always said, whoever you have a child with you should marry and now look. If that is my kid, Riley damn sure won't be my wife.

"I'm a grown ass man Riley or did you forget that?" I heard knocking at the door.

"How did you get pregnant anyway? I thought you were on the pill." She remained silent.

"Oh now cat got your tongue." I chuckled.

"Before you open that door I wanna know right now if there's another woman." I laughed and walked over to her.

"Even if it were, what can you say?" I pushed the hair behind her ear.

"The day you walked in this house smelling like a man, we both became single. The difference is, I never cheated on you but I did find comfort elsewhere."

"WHAT?" I could see her eyes beginning to water.

"Yea she's pretty awesome too and in the bedroom, I have to say she's shocked me with the things she can do." I kissed her cheek and went to the door.

"You fucked her?"

"The same way you fucked that nigga and got pregnant." She ran in the other room screaming about something. I opened the door and my cousin Tionne stood there with an evil look on her face. I was shocked because she's never been here.

"You got a minute?"

"Actually, I'm on my way out. What's up?" I was about to close the door behind me when my ex yelled out.

"You're not going anywhere." I turned around and Riley had a gun pointed at me.

"What the fuck are you doing here?" Riley shouted when she noticed my cousin standing there. Now I was really confused because to my knowledge they didn't know one another.

"Bitch are you crazy?" Tionne started flipping out and pulled a gun outta her purse.

"What's going on?"

"That's what I came here to tell you Mazza."
"Shut the fuck up bitch. You don't know what you're talking about." Riley yelled. My cousin never got to tell me the reason she stopped by because the two of them went back and forth for a minute or two.

BOOM! BOOM! A gun went off and all I saw was blood pouring out on my floor. How the fuck did this happen?

"Where you going?" My mom asked as I packed my overnight bag. I've been staying here instead of the place Mazza purchased because I wanted him to help me decorate. Yes, he said it was all mine but I still wanted to include him for some reason. However, ever since the day he left, I hadn't spoken to him and my gut told me something was wrong.

"To Delaware to make sure Mazza's ok."

"Hold on." She ran out the room and met me in the living room with her stuff.

"What are you doing?"

"Um, I'm coming with you. After you told me how that bitch rolled up in your store, ain't no way I'm sending you alone." I laughed because no matter how old my mom is, she was still down for whatever.

"Fine. We're leaving in an hour."

"An hour?"

"Yes, an hour."

"Shit, the way you rushing I thought you were ready to go now."

"I'm gonna take a shower first because I'm not sure where to go and we'll most likely be driving for a while."

"Ok well let me grab some weed from Steph. You should be finished when I get back." I told her ok and locked the door behind her.

The entire time in the shower all I could think about was, if Mazza's ok. Granted, Tyler told me she saw him but if that's the case why isn't he answering for me? He claims we're a couple but how is that possible when we haven't spoken? All I know is he better have an explanation and if he's with that bitch, I'm done. One thing I won't do is play a fool for another man.

I stepped out the shower, started putting lotion on and heard banging outside the door. I figured it was my mom because she left the key and went to the door in just my towel. Projects or not, people around here don't bother us. My mom is the cool lady who everyone loves.

"What do you want?" I only had the door halfway opened.

"You. Get dressed."

"I'm not going anywhere with you." He pushed the door all the way open, grabbed my hand and led me in the back.

"I'm tired of playing these games with you. You're coming home and that's, that."

"Jordan please go. I don't have time for this." He pushed me in the corner and against the wall.

"I told you before to come home but your stubborn ass didn't listen. Now I'm forced to come get you."

"Move." I tried to push him but he didn't budge."

"This is what's going to happen Zia." He reached on the bed and picked my bra up.

"Put this on." I snatched it out his hand and put it on over top of the towel. I still wasn't comfortable dressing in front of him.

"You're coming home and we're gonna discuss our living arrangements." I scoffed up a laugh.

"Finish." He threw the rest of my clothes at me.

"Then we're gonna act like none of this ever happened and continue living like the happy couple we were."

"Jordan we weren't happy. If we were, you would've never slept with those other women."

"Fuck them Zia. They mean nothing." Why do all men say that after they're caught?

"Just go Jordan. This is ridiculous."

"Hurry up." He threw my sneakers at me like I meant nothing to him.

"Are you crazy?"

"You know what. You're taking too long." He grabbed me by the hair, wrapped it around his hand and drug me out the front door. It felt like he could snap my neck at anytime from the way he gripped it. I prayed someone would help but unfortunately, the only people outside were a few kids who should've been in the house. It wasn't late but it was for small kids their age. I tried to yell and he popped me in the mouth like a child.

"I'll snap your fucking neck if you open this car door." He slammed it shut, went on the driver's side, sat down, placed his hand on my thigh and peeled out the parking lot.

"We're about to be a family Zia." I didn't say anything as he placed a big ass rock on my finger. *This motherfucker is crazy.*

To Be Continued...

Made in United States
Orlando, FL
20 February 2022

14986790R00124